Dark Encounters

Dark Encounters

A Collection of Ghost Stories

William Croft Dickinson

Introduction by
Alistair Kerr

First published in Great Britain in 1963 by Harvill Press.
Hardback edition published in 2017 by Polygon.
This paperback edition published in 2019 by Polygon,
an imprint of Birlinn Ltd.

Birlinn Ltd
West Newington House
10 Newington Road
Edinburgh
EH9 1QS

www.polygonbooks.co.uk

1

ISBN 978 1 84697 513 4
eBook ISBN 978 0 85790 950 3

British Library Cataloguing-in-Publication Data
A catalogue record for this book is available on request
from the British Library.

Typeset by 3btype.com, Edinburgh

Contents

Introduction

William Croft Dickinson

Scotland is famous for its ghostly tales and traditions, so who better than a former professor of Scottish History at the University of Edinburgh to present them to a modern readership? William Croft Dickinson has many claims to distinction, but he was also a master of writing spine-chilling – occasionally macabre – stories of the supernatural. He introduces us to his friends and colleagues: historians, scientists, archaeologists and antiquaries, and we share their occult adventures. These are often frightening; sometimes life-threatening, as in *Return at Dusk*, and occasionally fatal, as in *The Eve of St Botulph*.

For serious students and aficionados of Scottish history, William Croft Dickinson (1897–1963) needs no introduction. He was arguably the most distinguished twentieth-century historian of Scotland. As John Imrie recalled in his 1966 memoir, Dickinson was the author, co-author or editor of many books on Scottish history, including *A New History of Scotland*. He edited for publication a large number of primary sources; especially old court books and burgh records, one of which was *The Fife Sheriff Court Book*. These records give a fascinating contemporary picture of Scottish society and culture. He was (to date) the longest-serving Fraser Professor of Scottish History and Palaeography at the

University of Edinburgh, occupying that Chair from 1944 until his death in 1963. A few months before he died he received the distinction of Commander of the Most Excellent Order of the British Empire (CBE) for his services to the discipline of history in the 1963 New Year Honours List.

Outside the university Dickinson served on the Scottish Records Advisory Council, as a Trustee of the National Library of Scotland, as a member of the former Royal Commission on the Ancient and Historical Monuments of Scotland (RCAHMS) and on the Councils of the Scottish History Society and the Stair Society, which is concerned with promoting knowledge of the history of Scots law. In the words of his successor, Professor Gordon Donaldson, 'His services to Scottish history were many, but none of them surpassed in importance his work on this *Review*'. The periodical in question was *The Scottish Historical Review*, in which Dickinson's first published work had appeared in 1922 and which he had revived and refounded in 1947.

Dickinson, however, was more than just a brilliant academic historian. He was also a first-rate university administrator; these two accomplishments do not necessarily go together. He was an accomplished lecturer and *raconteur*. He was also a man of action. Dickinson's MA degree course began in 1915 but he did not graduate, with a first in history and a medal in modern history, until 1921: the First World War interrupted his studies at St Andrews. In 1916 he volunteered for service with the Royal Highland Regiment (RHR), usually known as the Black Watch. He was later commissioned in the Machine Gun Corps. His courage and leadership won him the Military Cross for 'conspicuous gallantry and devotion to duty' in an action near Ypres in 1917. Dickinson remained something of the old soldier thereafter. He attributed his formidable organisational and administrative skills to his army training. While most of his students found him a sympathetic and even inspirational teacher, he was especially friendly to former servicemen, many of whom he taught after the Second World War.

After graduating, Dickinson worked for a time as assistant to the distinguished St Andrews historian, J. D. Mackie. He undertook postgraduate studies, resulting in a PhD, conferred in 1924. Academic posts were few in Scotland in the 1920s, so Dickinson gladly accepted when Sir William Beveridge, the Director of the London School of Economics and Political Science (LSE), offered him the administrative post of the LSE's Assistant Secretary, at which he proved to be a great success. Dickinson continued to visit Scotland to attend relevant conferences (and play golf) and to write articles and books on Scottish history. He spent most of the Second World War until 1944 as the LSE's Librarian. In that year he took up his Professorial Chair in Edinburgh. In 1952 St Andrews would confer on him an Honorary Doctorate of Laws (LLD).

Despite his many admirable qualities, Dickinson had his critics; for a start, he was by no means politically correct. His English Nonconformist upbringing had influenced him to take a perceptibly Protestant partisan approach to some historical topics, including the Scottish Reformation. He had adapted happily to the Church of Scotland and became extremely knowledgeable about Scottish church history, editing John Knox's *History of the Reformation in Scotland*. This was one of his favourite subjects, on which he lectured pungently and with verve. Reportedly there was once a walk-out by Roman Catholic students in protest at some of his remarks. Dickinson's first ghost story, published in *Blackwood's Magazine*, seems to show empathy with the seventeenth-century Covenanters, which Scottish Episcopalians and Catholics might not necessarily share. It is nonetheless an excellent ghost story.

Second, Dickinson chose to write fiction, including ghost stories, as well as history. Some of his colleagues disapproved of his fiction writing; it is not entirely clear why. The reason may be that many historians prefer to read factual accounts of what really happened rather than imaginary ones describing what might, could or ought to have occurred, and it must be admitted that the historic reality is sometimes more interesting and bizarre than any novelist's imagination; you literally could not invent it. Moreover historians do not like to appear to endorse popular superstitions and other unverified traditions, even by indirect association.

Third, Dickinson was undeniably English, without any known Scots ancestry. This could have counted against him, at least in the early days. He had been born in Leicester, brought up in Yorkshire and educated at Mill Hill prior to his studies at St Andrews. He nevertheless knew far more about Scottish history than most birthright Scots: he taught the subject, researched it and wrote extensively about it. Despite this, even now lecturers and historians are apt occasionally to say and write that 'Dickinson was a great authority on Scottish History, although he was in fact English', as though that were slightly incongruous. Yet English people lecturing in Scottish universities – and vice-versa – are hardly unusual: would they have made that point if he had been lecturing and writing about, for example, African or Ancient History? In reality Dickinson had become thoroughly Scots at an early stage. His first year at St Andrews was probably the start of his love affair with Scotland and its past. His wartime service, initially with the Black Watch, helped the process of assimilation.

Dickinson seems to have belonged to a particular type of Englishman – perhaps more common in the past than now – who, often from an early age, identifies strongly and inexplicably with another people or culture. In some cases the identification is so strong as almost to suggest the possibility of reincarnation; of having genuinely belonged to that nation in a past life. This type, in cases where the country of their elective affinity was Scotland, could sometimes be encountered serving in the old Highland Infantry Regiments, like the Black Watch, which they had joined, *inter alia*, in order to wear the kilt. Other examples of this phenomenon include the late Dr Patrick Barden, who was born in Eastbourne but who became a distinguished Scot, a well-known herald painter and a breeder of pedigree Highland cattle; Hugh Dormer DSO, who had a visceral attachment to France, where he was killed in 1944; and Captain Robert Nairac GC, whose deep emotional involvement with Ireland was a factor in his murder there in 1977.

Dickinson's interest in writing fiction probably received encouragement as a result of his marriage in 1930 to Florence Tomlinson, the daughter of H.M. Tomlinson, who was then a well-known novelist, journalist, and biographer of Norman Douglas (although Dickinson's own first published fiction would not appear until 1944). Their only daughter, Susan Dickinson, would become a woman of letters, a publisher and a collector and editor of ghost stories, including her father's.

Dickinson wrote three novels for children: *Borrobil* (1944), *The Eildon Tree* (1947) and *The Flag from the Isles* (1951). They received critical acclaim and have been compared to the children's novels of Dickinson's contemporaries C.S. Lewis and J.R.R. Tolkien, although they are now out of print and less well known than the Narnia books or *The Hobbit*. Dickinson's novels, although all three contain magical, mystical or occult elements, were intended to awaken an interest in Scottish history in their young readers.

Historical novels for younger readers are one thing: many young people have been inspired to study history, having first read historical fiction by Kipling, G.A. Henty or Rosemary Sutcliffe, so they arguably serve a useful purpose. Ghost stories are another matter; some scholars perceive them as not quite intellectually respectable and as belonging to a literary *demi-monde*. At best they may be seen as a hobby-genre for the diversion of serious writers like Dickens or Henry James. Dickinson did not agree; in his view ghost stories, legends and superstitions were of legitimate interest to historians, forming part of the historical narrative and providing insights into the popular culture of the period. His interest in ghost stories was stimulated by the folk legends that he unearthed in the course of his researches and travels around Scotland. Dickinson's opinion shows how authentically Scots he had become: Scots, like other Celts, tend to treat the paranormal or supernatural as part of the natural order of things. Belief in such phenomena as the second sight is not confined to poorly educated people living in remote rural areas; it seems still to be widespread. Appropriately, the Koestler Parapsychology Unit, which studies alleged psychic phenomena among other things, has since 1985 been based within the University of Edinburgh.

That being so, it is not surprising that there should be an ancient and respectable tradition of composing ghost stories in Scotland. It goes back to pre-literate days, when a brilliant storyteller, especially if he were also a poet or minstrel, was equally welcome in the peasant's hut or the nobleman's castle. That tradition survived well within living memory: for example, it was common for older family members to tell ghost stories, or recite ghostly poems, to their children, grandchildren, nephews and nieces around the fire at Christmas and on other winter nights, to give them a pleasurable fright. Even after most of the population had become literate, this custom continued; as recently as the nineteenth and early twentieth centuries, many published ghost stories were clearly intended to be read aloud, especially at Christmas.

Because of this rich tradition, many of Scotland's finest authors have tried their hand at writing ghost stories. Two of the most spine-chilling ones ever written, *The Tapestried Chamber* and *Wandering Willie's Tale*, came from the pen of no less a wordsmith than Sir Walter Scott. Others who have done so include James Hogg (the Ettrick Shepherd); Mrs Margaret Oliphant, author of *The Open Door* and other stories; Robert Louis Stevenson; Sir

Arthur Conan Doyle (born in Edinburgh and a graduate of the University of Edinburgh, albeit of Irish descent); John Buchan, George Mackay Brown and, unexpectedly, Muriel Spark. Ian Rankin, the author of the Rebus detective novels, has his moments of supernatural spookiness, too. By choosing to write ghost stories, Dickinson placed himself firmly within a well-established Scottish literary tradition. All of his ghost stories take place within his adopted country of Scotland.

The next question is: what stimulated Dickinson to start writing ghost stories? The timing may offer a clue. His first one, entitled 'A Professor's Ghost Story', appeared in *Blackwood's Magazine* in 1947, three years after Dickinson had moved to Edinburgh, and it attracted favourable comment. Six years later, in 1953, it was reissued under a new name as the title story in a collection of four ghost stories: *The Sweet Singers and Three Other Remarkable Occurrents*, published by Oliver & Boyd and illustrated with atmospheric engravings by Joan Hassall. Copies of this book, its cover decorated with an austerely attractive post-war design, are uncommon and collectable. The flattering publisher's note explains that:

> We have come to expect much from our scholars and scientists, but it is seldom that we can greet them on common ground. Here we have a group of ghost stories having a background such as only the scholar can provide. Neat and compact, told with great charm and an undoubted flair, these stories make us realize that old shades can have new mystery when related to our present day and age.
>
> Each has its own 'atmosphere' – a word that has a fatal attraction for the antiquary in 'The Eve of St Botulph'. Each is based upon some known fact or episode in Scotland's past; but in each the past disturbs the present by a 'Return at Dusk' in some questionable shape.
>
> The opening story, 'The Sweet Singers', which has as its background the imprisonment of the Covenanters on the Bass

Rock, was widely acclaimed when printed some six years ago in
Blackwood's Magazine.

The second story, which is not mentioned in the publisher's note,
is 'Can These Stones Speak?'. It is set in an unnamed Scottish
university town, which might be Aberdeen or St Andrews, and
involves a horrible episode of time travel by an academic, who
unwillingly witnesses the immurement – the walling-in – of a
live, and presumably sexually incontinent, nun during the Middle
Ages. The fourth and last story, 'Return at Dusk', is in many
readers' view the most frightening. The Second World War is in
progress and the army has requisitioned an old Scottish castle
for a secret project. A young officer is posted to the castle,
innocently unaware that he is descended from the baronial
family who formerly lived there and that waiting for him is the
vengeful ghost of an hereditary enemy. The scene is now set for
supernatural mayhem and Dickinson does not disappoint.

From their dates of publication, it seems that his return to
Scotland, or at any rate the research that he undertook after his
arrival, stimulated Dickinson to start writing his ghost stories.
He would discover many sinister tales in the course of his travels
all over Scotland on behalf of the RCAHMS, but in truth he did
not need to look far beyond his own workplace and home area.
Edinburgh, according to ghost hunters, is the most haunted city
in the UK apart from London, which is considerably larger.

There are many Edinburgh ghost tales; they keep the
operators of 'ghost tour' companies gainfully employed during
the summer months. The castle is haunted; the palace is haunted.
So are many other places. According to legend, the unlucky
belated pedestrian risks encountering a tall, black-cloaked man
in the costume of a bygone age, whose carved walking-stick
hops ahead of him down the pavement, any time after midnight
in the West Bow. That ancient thoroughfare is near both the
university and George IV Bridge, where Dickinson bought his

pipe tobacco from Macdonald the tobacconist. The ghost is the shade of Major Thomas Weir (1599–1670), an evil seventeenth-century commander of the Town Guard, who escorted Montrose to the scaffold and was later executed in his turn as a self-confessed warlock and murderer, having previously been regarded as an exceptionally devout Presbyterian. (He may also have been an original of *Dr Jekyll and Mr Hyde*; Robert Louis Stevenson was familiar with his story.) A Victorian anatomist in a black frock-coat frequents the former Medical School at night. Greyfriars, the University Church, has one of the most interesting and numinous graveyards in the UK. Many famous and notorious people lie there; I hesitate to write "repose". They include Sir George Mackenzie of Rosehaugh (1636/38–1691), nicknamed 'The Bluidy Mackenzie', who supposedly does not rest quietly in his grand mausoleum. Mackenzie was in reality a distinguished lawyer, a highly cultured and much maligned man who backed the wrong political horse in 1688, but in popular myth he has become the demonic Scots equivalent of Judge Jefferies of the Bloody Assize, who is also the subject of ghost stories.

Sometimes the ghosts can become a positive nuisance; for example, according to Sir Walter Scott, the exasperated owners of Major Weir's former residence had it pulled down in 1830 because it had become a liability. The building was so disagreeably haunted that latterly nobody would live in it, not even if they were paid to do so.

The Dickinsons settled in Fairmilehead, which is now a leafy suburb but was then on the extreme southernmost edge of Edinburgh and still almost rural, with working farms nearby. There they generously entertained his students, although getting to Fairmilehead involved the undergraduates in a long journey by tram – latterly by bus – or bike from central Edinburgh. Outside the city boundary, but still within easy reach of Fairmilehead, were two of Scotland's most famous haunted locations: Woodhouselee, an old aristocratic country house, now owned by the university's Department of Agriculture, and Roslin Chapel and Castle.

Woodhouselee is said to be haunted, among others, by the ghost of Lady Anne Sinclair, a former owner's wife, who was evicted with her infant child in midwinter on the order of the then Regent of Scotland, James Stewart, Earl of Moray. They perished. It is said that their ghosts haunt the site and their screams can still be heard. Interestingly, the tragedy actually took place at Old Woodhouselee, several miles away and now an insignificant ruin. Many of its stones, however, were recycled to build the present Woodhouselee. The ghosts reportedly clung to the stones and continued to haunt the later house. In revenge, Lady Anne's widower, James Hamilton of Bothwellhaugh, stalked the Regent, finally ambushing him in Linlithgow in 1570. He fired a single shot at the Regent, leaving him with fatal wounds, and fled on horseback. This was the first recorded assassination by firearm.

Roslin is the scene of several authentic traditional ghost stories, one of which is related in Scott's poem *Rosabelle*, while another involves a gigantic spectral wolfhound, the Mauthe Dog, as well as more recent spurious legends invented by Dan Brown for *The Da Vinci Code*; a novel whose flagrant historical inaccuracies would have driven Dickinson up the wall.

It is likely that more than one writer influenced Dickinson's ghost stories, but the most obvious influence is that of Montague Rhodes James (M.R. James, 1862–1936), the author of *Ghost Stories of an Antiquary*, which is considered to include some of the most accomplished and terrifying ghost stories in English, including certain ones, like 'Count Magnus' and 'Whistle and I'll Come to You, My Lad', which have become internationally famous. *Ghost Stories of an Antiquary* has never gone out of print. Many of the stories have been adapted for film, television, radio or stage performance. Among other appointments, James served as Provost of King's College, Cambridge (1905–18) and of Eton

College (1918–36). Dickinson seems to have enjoyed James's stories. Given that he was working in London during the inter-war years, he might have met James, who survived until 1936, but I have seen no evidence that he ever did so; James, who was latterly a sick man suffering from cancer, lived a fairly reclusive existence at Eton. Dickinson had, however, visited Cambridge; it is possible that he became acquainted there with some of James's friends and former colleagues. A few clues in his stories might imply this.

There are undoubted similarities between James's and Dickinson's style and content. This has led some critics to regard Dickinson as little more than a member of James's 'school', writing in careful and derivative imitation of his master. That does not do justice to Dickinson's originality, although both authors used an elegant, understated and scholarly style, as though they were narrating genuine historical events for well-educated and well-informed readers. Both could faultlessly reproduce the prose of past eras. The most terrifying conclusions are seldom spelled out; the reader is often left to work out what must have happened and the penny can take a few moments to drop. Both authors tend to use realistic contemporary settings, at least at the start of their stories. They may subsequently travel back in time. In several Dickinson stories the narrative begins with a group of academics reminiscing in front of the fire in the Edinburgh University Staff Club, which was then located in the Old College. Something suddenly prompts one of them to recount a curious tale . . . In M.R. James's stories the academics' conversation takes a similar turn, but the location is the High Table or Combination Room of an ancient Cambridge college.

Both authors have a tendency to involve real people, objects, places and historic events in their ghost fiction, which adds to its air of authenticity. In Dickinson's case one story, 'The Witch's Bone', centres on a magical relic or talisman which is kept in a museum. The National Museum of Scotland possesses such a bone and, although it is not on display, Dickinson evidently knew of it and wrote a story about it. In 'The Sweet Singers' mention is made of a real rare book, *Jehovah Jireh* (1643), a copy of which is held by the University Library. Another rare book, allegedly held in the same library, appears in 'The Work of Evil'. I have not sought it out; it is apparently a magical treatise that brings early death to people foolish enough to consult it.

Although Dickinson gave the real locations of some of his stories – 'The Eve of St Botulph' takes place among the ruins of Dundrennan Abbey, for example – in other stories he does not. Readers can have fun trying to work out the location in these cases. 'Quieta non Movere', aka 'The Black Dog of Wolf's Crag', is in fact set at Fast Castle in East Lothian, but Sir Walter Scott had renamed Fast Castle 'Wolf's Crag' in his novel *The Bride of Lammermuir*, so Dickinson decided to use that name. Joan Hassall's illustrations and hints dropped by Dickinson himself suggest that he had the picturesque Craigievar Castle in mind for the castle in 'Return at Dusk', although this building – formerly a Forbes family residence and now a National Trust for Scotland property – was never requisitioned by the army. It is, however, home to several ghosts and is the scene of one particular ghost legend that resembles the terrifying legend in 'Return at Dusk'. Although Craigievar was inhabited and therefore not open to the public until after 1963, the year of Dickinson's death, he evidently visited it and learned about their legend from the Forbes family or from local people.

There are, however, important differences between James's and Dickinson's work. They belonged to different generations, having been born thirty-five years apart. A vast gulf of experience separated them because Dickinson served in the Great War and James, who was fifty-two in 1914, did not. James's historical consciousness appears to have stopped at the latest in about 1910. Although he lived until 1936 and even after 1918 he continued to improve and edit his stories for republication;

occasionally writing, or starting to write, new ones to add to the canon, James took little notice of the changes that had happened in England since August 1914. Some of his stories take place as long ago as the seventeenth or eighteenth, but for the most part they happen in the latter half of the nineteenth or in the early twentieth centuries. England is seated amid honour and plenty; still the richest country on Earth. The country houses are intact; their old families still usually live in them, although *nouveaux riches* may occasionally rent or acquire them. Following some alarming psychic disturbance, they sometimes end by wishing that they had not. Dons and clergymen occupy an honoured position in society. Trains are frequent and reliable; characters living in the depths of the country can easily 'run up to London' for a day in order to consult a book in a library, visit the British Museum or talk to an expert. The strong pound Sterling gives gentlemen antiquaries a favourable exchange rate, allowing them to travel at leisure and in comfort around an unspoiled Europe, where their researches, begun in all innocence, are apt to place them in danger. France, Germany and the Low Countries are easily accessible; Scandinavia and other regions seem more remote and exotic.

By contrast, only a few of Dickinson's stories take place earlier than the Second World War, although they often have echoes from an earlier period, which can suddenly come back to life and may prove lethal. The main action normally happens in the 1940s, 1950s or the very early 1960s. Dickinson's characters tend to have served in one or both World Wars. Academics now live frugally and pass their holidays playing golf, hill-walking or on archaeological digs in Scotland.

Dickinson lived into the early computer age and was aware of its possibilities; the University of Edinburgh was in the forefront of the development of artificial intelligence and no doubt the latest developments were excitedly discussed in the University Staff Club. He wrote at an interesting moment in the development of the supernatural story: when it started to embrace modern science, including computers and psychology. The distinction between ghost stories and science fiction was becoming slightly blurred. Thus he bridges the gap between M.R. James and modern writers like Ray Russell and Stephen King.

In one of the last of Dickinson's ghost stories, 'His Own Number' (1963), related by a professor of geography, an evil spirit becomes computer-literate and predicts the precise location and grid reference of a technician's death, which it causes. There is a comparable and apparently authentic computer ghost story – or urban legend – about one of the older Cambridge Colleges. Using a computer, the ghost issues warnings and threats which are more explicit than those in 'His Own Number'. To date it has reportedly killed two people who disregarded them and the college has banned any further research on the subject: as a result, I have been unable to discover when the alleged hauntings are supposed to have begun. If it should prove that they started after 1963, clearly Dickinson could not have been aware of them or have used them in his story, but it is still an intriguing coincidence. Details may be found in *Cambridge College Ghosts* by Geoff Yeates (Jarrold, 1994).

Although Dickinson's admirers consider that, at his best, he was as good as M.R. James, their posthumous literary fortunes have been different. William Croft Dickinson's reputation as a Scottish historian remains immense, while his ghost stories, despite their merits, are now largely forgotten. By contrast M.R. James has achieved international fame on the basis of *Ghost Stories of an Antiquary*, while his important work as a mediaevalist and biblical scholar, including an invaluable English edition of the Apocryphal New Testament, is unknown to most people. This may irritate his ghost but on the other hand, until the copyright expired, *Ghost Stories of an Antiquary* and the various adaptations for stage and cinema must have been a wonderful source of revenue for his estate.

While M.R. James or his literary agent had marketed *Ghost Stories of an Antiquary* professionally – collecting them into four volumes, later two, and finally one, and occasionally bringing out new, improved and expanded editions – that did not happen to Dickinson's ghost stories. This may reflect the fact that, as the holder of a professorial chair and having many other commitments, he simply did not have much time to devote to promoting his works of fiction. After he published *The Sweet Singers and Three Other Remarkable Occurrents* in 1953, no further collections appeared until the first edition of *Dark Encounters*, which Dickinson edited on his deathbed and which brought together almost all of Dickinson's ghost stories. It was published posthumously by Harvill Press in 1963.

In the interim Dickinson continued to write ghost stories; they appeared in magazines and in the Christmas issues of *The Scotsman*. Dickinson had undertaken to write a ghost story for that Edinburgh newspaper every year, starting in 1957. He did so until 1963; his last story, 'The MacGregor Skull', was published posthumously that year. The invitation to provide the annual Christmas ghost story was flattering but, as December began to draw near, inspiration sometimes proved elusive; the story, however, still had to be written. The quality of Dickinson's last stories is uneven; a few seem slightly to lack spontaneity. Nevertheless the series was judged to have been a great success. It continued for many years after Dickinson's death, with other well-known writers, such as George Mackay Brown, writing the ghost stories. An obvious drawback to publication in a periodical was that the stories were read and admired at the time but the magazine or newspaper was later discarded and the story forgotten.

A further possible reason for the stories' eclipse may be that Dickinson set all of them in Scotland, so they might have become unfairly pigeon-holed in critics' and publishers' minds as 'Scottish interest only'. That ought not to be counted against them, but by contrast M.R. James's tales take place in England – especially his beloved East Anglia – France, Sweden, Denmark and Germany. This may have given them a wider appeal.

'The MacGregor Skull' was missed out of *Dark Encounters* in 1963 because it was due to appear in *The Scotsman* at Christmas that year. It was omitted again in 1984, probably through an oversight, when *Dark Encounters* was republished by Wendover Goodchild with an introduction by Susan Dickinson. No further editions have appeared, although individual Dickinson stories have occasionally been included in anthologies of ghost stories, some of which Susan Dickinson edited; for example, in *The Armada Book of Ghost Stories*.

Now that you know something of the author's distinguished career, your next question is likely to be: 'Have his stories stood the test of time?' I think so: the proof of the pudding is in the eating. A few years ago I was house-sitting for a friend, alone in an old Georgian house in an ancient cathedral town. One gloomy evening, when there was nothing of interest on television, I made the grave error of reading some of Dickinson's ghost stories, which I had not read for many years, from my host's extensive library of detection, mystery and horror. I found that they still had the power to raise the hair on the back of my neck; especially 'Return at Dusk'. I did not get much sleep that night.

A new edition of *Dark Encounters* has long been overdue: I feel honoured to have been invited to write the introduction to these powerful stories. Enjoy them!

The Keepers of the Wall

The Keepers of the Wall

'I SEE THAT someone has discovered a number of skeletons beneath the foundations of a wall and has brought forward the old idea that they were put there so that their ghosts could hold up the wall.'

'And why not?' interposed Henderson. 'It was long thought that burying a body under a wall would help to hold the wall secure.'

'Didn't Gordon Childe find something like that at Skara Brae?' queried Drummond.

'Yes,' Henderson confirmed. 'He found the skeletons of two old women at the foot of one of the walls; but he made only a suggestion that possibly they had been buried there so that their ghosts could hold up the wall. A guess, if you like. But a good guess.'

'I could tell you of a much more modern instance,' put in Robson, our new Professor of Mediaeval Archaeology. And I noticed that he spoke hesitantly. 'A sixteenth-century instance. Ghosts to hold up a wall. Perhaps even ghosts to gather the living to help them in their task,' he added slowly. 'Don't ask me to explain what I mean by that. I just don't know. All I know is that recently I had a terrifying experience on the west coast – an experience that still makes me frightened of visiting ancient ruins by night.'

'I once had a terrifying experience myself,' said Drummond, quietly. 'You'll find at least one listener who'll understand. And the oftener you tell a tale, the less it haunts you.'

'Well, perhaps I'll find some of your relief, Drummond, by telling you the story of my night in the castle of Dunross – in March of this year, just before I came to Edinburgh to take up my chair.'

———··✦··———

As you probably know, Dunross is one of a small group of interesting twelfth-century stone castles on the western sea-board. Only one of its sea-walls still stands, right up to the original wall-head (a feature which I now know only too well); the other two sea-walls have fallen down the cliff in a cascade of stones to the sea. The remaining wall, the landward wall, is little more than a few feet high, ruined and broken, though in it there is an entrance-gate with the remains of a stone stairway that undoubtedly rose up to the wall-walk. The better-known and better-preserved castles of Kisimul, Mingary and Tioram, each of them, like Dunross, perched on a sea rock, follow much the same plan; and I had a theory that the siting, the plan, and the constructional details of all four were so closely related that they bespoke the work of one particular school of military architects. Because of that, I had decided to make a careful examination of Dunross to confirm my belief that it fitted into the general plan of the group.

Right at the start I was fortunate enough to find a crofter living by himself in a good-sized house some two or three miles from the castle. He had more than one room to spare, and he was more than willing to put me up. Moreover, he seemed to take a keen interest in my work, and came to join me every evening so that we could go home from Dunross together. And, as we walked back to his house, I would burden him with architectural details in which, as I was to learn in the end, he took no interest whatsoever.

I had appreciated his regular evening call, and had looked upon it as a friendly act. I had also appreciated our regular walk home. But when, on the night prior to my departure, I told him I would have to make one last visit to the castle in order to check a detail of the entrance-gate which I had not entered clearly enough in my note-book, I discovered he had had a definite reason of his own for calling to pick me up at the end of each day's work.

'You will not be going to Dunross in the night?' he asked, as I prepared to set out.

'Why, yes,' I replied. 'I just want to check a detail of the entrance-gate. I'll soon be back; and I have a torch. But don't wait up for me.'

'You cannot go there after the dark,' he replied, fiercely. 'It would be madness. You would not come back. The wall would shut you in.'

I looked at him with astonishment. 'The wall would shut me in,' I repeated, lamely.

'Just so,' he answered. 'And for why would you think I have brought you away every evening as the darkness was closing in? Was it not to make sure you would not be kept there, like the rest of them? Shut in by the wall, to help to hold it firm.'

'To hold what wall firm? And how?' I asked, more mystified still. 'And who are "the rest", anyway?'

'You did not know, then?'

I shook my head.

'It is the ghosts of the MacLeods,' he replied. 'And since you do not know, I must tell you what way it is.'

And thereupon he told me a strange tale that, away back in the past, when there was a long-standing feud between the MacLeods and the MacDonalds of Clanranald, the MacDonalds had seized a birlinn, manned by MacLeods, and had brought the boat and their prisoners to Dunross. It was a time when MacDonald himself was rebuilding one of the sea-walls of his castle. So what did MacDonald do? Some of the MacLeods were just thrown into the dungeons, and left to starve there till they died; but six of them, fine strong fellows, were buried at the foot of MacDonald's new wall so that their ghosts would hold it secure. And that, I was told, was the one sea-wall which still stood, with never a stone that had fallen from it. Had I not seen it for myself? The other walls were ruined and tumbled down. But the ghosts of the six MacLeods would always hold that one sea-wall secure and strong.

'Well, that may be so,' I answered, when he had finished. 'But I still don't see why it should be dangerous to go to Dunross by night. As long as those ghosts are holding up the wall it can hardly fall down on me.'

'May be so!' he repeated, his eyes flashing. 'I tell you, man, it is so. No one has gone to Dunross by night and returned again. The MacLeods are wearying of their work and aye seeking others to share with them the burden of the wall.'

'And so evening visitors have been compelled to stay on,' I rejoined. And probably there was a little banter in my tone.

'I have told you the tale of it,' he replied, with Highland dignity. 'My father knew it, and his father before him. And, for a truth, they told me of two men who did not return. One, I mind, was a shepherd, seeking a ewe that had strayed; the other was a young man like yourself, who had come from the south and who would not be believing in ghosts and in walls that could shut a man in.'

With that parting shot he left me, to attend to some small task of his own. I could see that my disbelief had offended him, but I knew that the hurt would soon pass. But what of his tale? Of course I didn't believe it. And yet, for a brief space, I did hesitate about my final visit to Dunross. In the end I decided to go. Walls simply did not shut one in; and probably every Scottish castle had its ghost. Moreover, I did not want to leave without checking that detail of the entrance-gate.

'A typical legend,' I muttered to myself as I slipped on my oilskin. I felt my torch in my pocket. I had that, anyway. I opened the door quietly and stepped out into the night.

I must admit that as I walked along the rough track that led to Dunross I was by no means as carefree as I would have been had my host not told his tale. I was ready to start at every shadow, and when, at last, I saw the dim outline of the ruined castle ahead of me, I stopped and very nearly turned back. But that reference to the 'young man from the south who did not believe in ghosts' acted as a challenge. I would go on and check that detail of the entrance-gate. More than that, I would go up to MacDonald's sea-wall, give it a resounding slap with my hand, say 'Good-bye' to the ghosts of the MacLeods, and then return to my host and tell him what I had done.

I walked boldly up to the castle. With the aid of my torch I studied the detail of the ruined entrance-gate. Then, sitting down on the grass, I propped my torch against a stone and made the necessary additional drawings in my note-book. By the time I had finished, all my misgivings had passed. I got up, shone my torch ahead of me, and marched boldly through the entrance-gate, across the castle-court, and straight up to the one high-standing and unbroken sea-wall.

'So much for ghosts,' I said aloud, as I stood a few feet from the wall, playing my torch up and down its length. And, at that very instant, my torch went out.

It would be idle to pretend that I was not frightened. I half-turned, and was on the point of running back to the entrance-gate, when I pulled myself together. A wall was a wall, and nothing more. Moreover, although the night was not completely black, I realized that I might easily stumble over one or more of the many fallen stones in the castle-court – and possibly sprain an ankle, perhaps even break a leg. And what should I do then?

'Don't be a fool,' I remember saying to myself. 'Have a look at your torch.'

The battery had given no previous indication that it was running down. Probably there was simply a faulty contact. I struck the torch gently against the palm of my hand. Nothing happened. Somewhat anxiously I struck it this way and that, again and again. Still it refused to work. The answer could only be that the filament in the bulb had broken. 'Damn the thing,' I said, and stuffed it back into my pocket. I would have to crawl on all fours to the entrance-gate. Safer that way. And I would get some assistance from the faint light in the sky.

Then I remembered my matches! I opened the box carefully and felt inside. Good! There were quite a number left. Certainly enough to light my way through the fallen stones. And there was no wind.

I took out a match and struck it; but it failed to light. Thinking I had struck the wrong end of the match, I turned it round in my fingers and again struck it on the box. Still no light came. Throwing the match away, I took out another. Again the match refused to light. Frenziedly, and with shaking hands, I tried match after match, but not one would strike. I came to the last match of all. I prayed that it would strike. But there was still the same hard scrape on the sandpaper of the box, and no welcome blaze of light.

After that, it is difficult to tell you what happened. To say that I was now frightened would be an understatement. I was terrified. Yet somehow I still kept myself under control. Almost as soon as I had thrown away my last match I dropped down on to my hands and knees, turned my back to the wall, and began to crawl away as fast as I could. In that way, I assured myself, I was bound to find the entrance-gate in time. And pray heaven it would not take long.

I had crawled perhaps twenty yards when I came to fallen stones. That meant I was now well away from the wall. I looked up, hoping to see the low ruins of the landward-wall silhouetted against the sky. Instead, I saw in front of me the high-towering unbroken sea-wall from which I had fled.

At once I turned and crawled away in the opposite direction. Smooth turf! Fallen stones! Ah! I was away this time. And this time, as I looked up, slowly and fearfully, again I saw the sea-wall barring my way.

With that, I'm not ashamed to say that all my control went. For some reason or other – possibly a subconscious fear of disabling myself on the fallen stones – I did not stand up and run. I scurried on all fours, first this way, then that, constantly looking for the escape that would be offered by the broken outline of the landward-wall and as constantly seeing only the high unbroken sea-wall in front of me.

How long that lasted I do not know. I had lost all sense of time. Perhaps I had lost all reason too. All I know is that, in the end, bruised, weary, and utterly worn out, I sat down. I was resigned to my fate. If the wall had to close in upon me, if I had to disappear as the others had done, well, let it be so. I could do no more.

And then, when all hope had gone, even when all desire had gone with it, I heard the sound of crunching stones. This was the end. It came almost as a relief. But, strangely, no stones crushed me. I suffered no entombment, no agony in which I fought for breath. Instead, a bright light suddenly burned on my closed and waiting eyes. What did this final torture mean?

Summoning up all the last dregs of courage that were left in me, I opened my eyes, slowly, wearily, painfully. The light dazzled me. Then, with a queer feeling that I didn't know whether to shout, or to laugh, or to cry, I realised that I was in the beam from the headlights of a car – headlights that were shining through the entrance-gate, and shining straight on to me. I heard a shout; then another. Seconds later, I was literally carried out of the castle and gently lifted into the car. Someone poured a stiff whisky down my throat. And a blessed uncon-sciousness came to me.

The next morning I awoke in my own bed. My host, the crofter, was sitting on a chair by the bedside. He must have heard me move, for he stood up and bent over me.

'You'll be feeling fine now,' he said, half in question, half in affirmation.

I looked up at him, my wits slowly recovering.

'I am glad you came,' I said, slowly. 'I was all in, and ready to die. It seemed as though the wall would never let me go.'

'Praised be the Lord, but we cheated it. The doctor and I. The two of us. No less. For I had not the boldness to be seeking you at Dunross by my own self.'

There was the sound of a car outside.

'And there's the doctor, now,' he cried, striding quickly to the door.

The doctor was middle-aged, keen-eyed, and carrying himself like an athlete.

'So here is the young man who doesn't believe in ghosts,' he said cheerily, as he came over to my bed. 'Don't know that I do myself. Can't be sure.'

He took my wrist and felt the beating of my pulse.

'Not bad at all,' he said. 'Fine, in fact, for the morning after the night before. Did I say I didn't believe in ghosts? Or do I? Don't know. Yet I doubt if I'd go to Dunross by night. Save when called out on duty, of course.'

His eyes were twinkling, and his whole manner was a tonic and restorative.

'Tell me now,' he continued, 'what happened to ye before we picked ye up. And once we were carrying ye to my car, there ye were, sobbing like an unhappy child.'

'I didn't know that,' I replied.

'It helps, man. It helps. Washes away the worries. But what happened to ye?'

Haltingly I told him of the sudden failure of my torch, of the matches that would not strike, and of the wall always in front of me, always shutting me in.

'So,' he said, when I had finished. 'So that is the way of it. I've often wondered what those dead MacLeods did to their evening visitors. But man, I suspect ye were just crawling in circles. 'Tis easy enough. And easier still when terror gets hold of ye. Have ye ever tried to find the door of a room, in the black-out, when the bombs started dropping down?'

'But my torch!' I cried. 'My matches!'

'Do ye put spent matches back into the box, tidy-like, instead of throwing them away?' he asked.

Here was a thought that sobered me. But it was impossible.

'Yes,' I admitted, grudgingly. 'But only occasionally. There could not possibly be more than two or three spent matches in the box at any time. And even if all the matches were spent ones – and I'm convinced they were not – what of my torch? Why did that fail, too?'

'Let me look at it,' he said.

'It will be in the pocket of my oilskin,' I replied, raising myself up and looking around the room. 'There, on the peg by the door.'

He walked over to my oilskin and took out the torch. He pressed the switch, and at once the torch shone bright and clear.

For a moment or two he hummed a tune to himself. He tried the torch a second time; and once more it lit at his touch.

'So,' he said again. 'Yet I've known the horn on my car fail to sound one day and sound like the last trump on the day following.'

Again he hummed his tune as he played with my torch in his

hand. Then the movement of his hand slackened. The humming ceased. He dropped the torch on a chair and turned to me. And this time there was a different look in his eyes.

'Man, but I'm afraid,' he said, slowly. 'We've been playing with explanations because we feared the circumstance. Did I say I would not go to Dunross by night? I doubt I shall not be going to Dunross by day, either. To be frank with ye, I dare not go. I dare not go, lest I should find there an answer that is no answer – lest I should find a cluster of live matches lying there, at the foot of the wall.'

Return at Dusk

Return at Dusk

'YES,' I HEARD Drummond saying with emphasis, 'for the rest of my life I shall endeavour to avoid looking into a mirror at twilight.'

For a moment there was dead silence in the Common Room. We were all gazing at Drummond with surprise. That our Professor of Anthropology should be afraid of looking into a mirror at twilight seemed too absurd to be believed. And I well remember my own confused medley of thoughts in which I found myself trying to reconcile Drummond (tall, broad-shouldered, and of noted physical courage) with a mirror and some strange masculine version of the Lady of Shalott.

Drummond must have noticed the silence. He turned round, apologetically. 'But it's true,' he continued, in a quieter voice, and this time speaking to all of us. 'A mirror at twilight worries me. I never know what I may see in it.'

'Something to do with Black Magic and your African adventures?' asked MacEwen, peering over his spectacles with excited eyes, and hoping for another of the astonishing (but well vouched-for) adventures which Drummond had experienced in his African field-work.

'No,' came the unexpected answer. 'Something to do with

history and with a place only about a hundred miles distant from this room.'

MacEwen leaned back, disappointed. But the rest of us leaned forward.

'Out with it,' ordered Forrester, bluntly. 'You've said both too much and too little to escape saying more.'

'Well, here it is then,' answered Drummond, 'though for reasons which you will soon appreciate you must forgive me if I change the names of persons and places.'

———·◦✧◦·———

As you know, I was in Africa when the war broke out. The news, when it reached me, was about a fortnight old, and I promptly trekked south to join the nearest regiment I could find. It seemed the simplest thing to do. But I might just as well have made for the coast and a boat home, for, within a week of becoming a private in the South African Rifles, I was suddenly summoned to Headquarters and there told to pack my traps forthwith. Apparently some anxious G.S.O. in the War Office had sent out a 'Search all Africa' order, with the rider that as soon as I had been found I was to be returned to London with all possible speed.

Well, to cut a long story short, I was flown to Cairo and two days later I was reporting to that selfsame anxious G.S.O. in his own doubly-guarded room in Whitehall. It was simply the old 1914–18 game once more. I was to take charge of one of the special sections devoted to counter-espionage.

But don't jump to conclusions. What I am going to tell you has nothing to do with enemy agents. All this is simply to explain how, for some six months in the winter of 1939–40, a small group of us came to be located in such an out-of-the-way place as Cairntoul Castle[1] in Mar. We were sent there by the War Office, that's all. Probably Cairntoul had been chosen because of the sheer unlikeliness of the choice; and certainly all the arrangements must have been made long before Hitler marched into Poland. The castle might be out-of-the-way, but, when we arrived there to take over, we found we were very much in touch with London and with the other sections doing similar work, and I need hardly say that our powerful transmitting and receiving set, with its aerial cunningly concealed in the old dovecot, was not installed overnight.

In addition to our two wireless engineers, two batmen-clerks (working in that dual capacity), and one cook, there were eight of us in the section. But the unlucky number thirteen was avoided by the presence of Mrs Lumsdaine, the old caretaker or retainer – probably an octogenarian – whom the War Office had taken over with the castle, though not, I expect, without full investigation into her character and into the characters of her forbears back to the ninth generation or more. The old lady was certainly sound enough, but whoever had had the task of taking over the castle must have found her a handful. Yet 'Mother Lum' (as we called her) kept pretty much out of our way. I could feel that she resented our intrusion into 'her' castle. To get more than two words out of her was like drawing water from a stone; but to get a cold searching look whenever our ways met was as common as porridge for breakfast on a Highland croft.

Actually, as I was to discover later, the old lady's attachment to Cairntoul was simply part of that old loyalty so characteristic of the Highlands. *We* were aliens, but *she* had been born into the service of the castle, just as her parents and their parents before them had been born into the same service and had served and died there. In earlier days, indeed, the castle must often have seen such loyal lifelong service, and, earlier still, service of a different kind when loyalty to the House probably meant dying in its defence, and dying long before the attainment of old age. The very stones emphasized that. The place was more than a castle, it was a 'strength'. Its massive structure was built in the shape of an L with the doorway in the re-entrant angle where it could be effectively defended from both wings. The old outer wooden door had been replaced by a modern one, but the inner 'iron yett' was still there. I can tell you, I wouldn't have liked the task of breaking in, for, even when the iron yett had been won, there was what we should now call a 'baffle-wall' which put the defenders in the shadow, darkened the whole entrance, and made it impossible for more than one man at a time to gain the staircase which wound upwards immediately behind the wall. Again, the staircase itself was narrow – about thirty inches wide, I should say – and, being helical, was lit only at odd intervals, so that again the defenders could choose the shadows to contest its passage. And only by that staircase could one get into the castle at all. The stone stairs, worn with age, led direct to the first floor, to a corner of the 'Hall' – a long room, fully thirty-five feet long, and probably fifteen feet wide – with another staircase at its further end leading down again to the ground floor and to the vaulted kitchens below that. In the chamber, in the shorter wing, adjoining the Hall, a newel staircase led to the second floor. Thus the main staircase had to be fought for and won, step by step, before the castle itself could be won. Altogether a thoroughly interesting old place, and one ideal for security, ancient or modern.

The ground floor and the vaulted kitchens were wholly given over to the signallers, the two batmen-clerks, and the cook; though Mother Lum had kept her own room on the ground floor, in the wing. The big Hall was our general workroom (with an overflow into the adjoining chamber), and our sleeping-quarters were upstairs on the second floor where, in the main wing, all the rooms led out of one another. In the shorter wing, however, there was one room only, larger than the rest, which had a second door leading outside to a kind of beacon-turret.

That room in the wing, called the Turret Room, was at first mine; and being one who likes to know what there may be behind doors, or where doors may lead to, I had opened the second door almost as soon as I had crossed the threshold of the room. But the turret outside was empty (save for a dead bird), and, being corbelled, it was clearly impossible for anyone to reach it from the ground below, whilst even if the impossible were achieved, an iron grille which completely enclosed the turret-top would effectively prevent the climber from entering the turret and so gaining access to the room.

All these ancient precautions, as I have said, were ideal for security; and, to remain inconspicuous, we had no sentry or armed guard of any kind. Nevertheless our signallers had fixed an electric contact to the iron yett (which it was our practice to keep shut), and a whole battery of bells rang throughout the building whenever that gate was opened. In addition, a further press-bell was hidden in the darkness of the baffle-wall and, on this, whenever any one of us had entered by the iron yett he gave a series of rings (the number being changed each day) so that the whole battery of bells again informed us that only one of our own number was entering our strength.

For a month or so after our arrival at Cairntoul we were kept busy for a good sixteen hours out of every twenty-four. As a team we worked well together; and although nominally I was in charge, our work was essentially co-operative. I need not add that that first spell of intensive work was not without its reward.

Then came two or three slightly less busy days, and for the first time I was able to arrange for each of us, singly, to get out on to the moors to stretch his legs or, if he liked, to laze in the yielding heather.

My own turn came last, and for a whole afternoon I lay deep in the heather, dozing, and drawing in physical and mental rest. Returning to Cairntoul, in the gathering twilight, I passed a few words with the others, who were busy in the Hall, before climbing the further flight of stairs to my Turret Room. I was still in a happy mood of complete content, and, once in my room,

I sat down on a chair, letting my mind absorb the quietness which seemed to be all around, bringing with it an air of peace so different from the work which we had just been doing and had still to do.

I had sat down on the chair in front of the table which served as a dressing-chest and over which an old mirror was hanging on the wall. Behind me was the door leading to the beacon-turret. Now what made me look up into the mirror, I cannot say. But look up I did, and, as I looked into the mirror, I saw that the door to the turret was slowly opening. I watched that opening door like one fascinated, and, somehow, I could neither move nor cry out. Slowly the opening grew wider and wider. Then a face appeared, peering round the side of the door. In the mirror, the face seemed to look straight into mine, but in the twilight I could recognize no features – just the blur of a face, that, and no more. Then the face withdrew, and the door began to close again, as slowly and as quietly as it had opened. It shut (though I could swear I heard no click of the latch), and, as soon as it had shut, the sense of powerlessness immediately left me. I felt suddenly and strangely released and, jumping up, I rushed towards the door. But, half-way, I stopped. Surely I had imagined it all. Probably my nerves had become too tightly stretched with that recent spell of intensive work. After all, one could dream by day as well as by night. Still, I'd better look into that beacon-turret, if only to satisfy myself. I took the few remaining steps, paused, and then quickly flung open the door. Nothing! This time not even a dead bird, for I had previously removed the one that had been there on my first arrival.

Wisely, or unwisely, I said nothing about my 'visitor'. But exactly ten days later, when the whole incident was beginning to fade from my mind, I was rudely brought back to reality, or unreality, and again at twilight. Again I was sitting in front of my dressing-chest, and this time I was certainly *not* dreaming. Actually I was brushing my hair before dinner, my mind alive and alert with the details of a pretty problem that had cropped up during the course of the day's work. And, in the midst of that simple operation of brushing my hair, my hands suddenly dropped. With a start, I had noticed in the mirror that the door to the beacon-turret was again opening, and opening as slowly and as quietly as it had opened before. Again an inquiring head peered round the side of the door. But this time it did not withdraw. The door opened wider and wider. The head was followed by a body. There was a quick movement, and my 'visitor' had entered the room: and I remember noting that the door seemed to swing-to and shut by itself.

Now, don't ask me what my 'visitor' looked like. I simply don't know. Partly the twilight was deepening into dusk, so that the light was poor; but mainly I seemed impelled to look only at the face which was reflected in my mirror. And that face, or perhaps I should say the eyes, held me as though I had been hypnotized. Never had I seen such concentrated hate before, and I hope I shall never see it again. As I have said, I seemed to be hypnotized, or, if you prefer it that way, I felt transfixed and powerless, just as I had felt before. Slowly, very slowly, almost as though I was to be taken by surprise, 'it' began to cross the intervening space, the eyes holding mine. That slow, deliberate closing-in was horrible. I was the victim of all the evil in the world which was now closing in for the kill. And I could do nothing. I felt a peculiar 'bristling' at the back of my neck – and I can assure you that 'hair-raising' is a phrase which is used too lightly and too often. It is not a pleasant sensation. Although I had been in many tight corners in my life, I think I may say that never before had I been terrified. But I was then. Unable to move, or even to cry out, my mind raced round and round the one question: what will it do when it reaches me? Probably everything took place in a matter of seconds, but to me the torment was protracted beyond the limits of endurance. Slowly that face approached behind me. Larger and larger in the mirror grew those awful eyes. Now I became convinced I could feel its breath upon me. A pair of hands seemed to reach out and close upon my neck. And . . . and all went black.

I am told that when I was abominably late for dinner, one of the others came up from the Hall to remind me of the time. He knocked on the door of my room and, receiving no answer, looked in. Thereafter, for a brief space there was some bustle and confusion in Cairntoul. But, as it was, it simply transpired that for the first time in my life I had fallen to the floor in a dead faint.

When at last they had brought me round I made some kind of feeble excuse – overwork or liver, or perhaps a combination of the two. I suppose I felt too ashamed to confess that I had fainted before a ghost. For, ponder over it as I could, no other explanation seemed possible. No alarm bell had rung; no one could reach that beacon-turret from the ground; and, above all, there was the iron grille. I remember spending that night sitting and dozing in front of the fire in the Hall, unwilling to return to my room. By morning I had ashamedly come to the conclusion that I couldn't face that room again.

As good luck would have it, however, that very morning brought the possibility of change. Just before lunch a coded message came through calling away one of my team on an urgent, but fortunately lengthy, task in Holland. It was a bit of a rush to get his papers ready and to get him to Aberdeen in time for the London express. But it took my mind from my visitor; also, and more important so far as I was concerned, it freed a room. Taking one of the batmen-clerks with me, I moved all my possessions into that providentially-provided spare room – making an excuse about an appalling draught that came from the beacon-turret.

What my team thought or guessed about my change of rooms, I do not know. But a chance meeting with Mother Lum a few days later seemed to reveal that there was a 'history' to Cairntoul not unconnected with the turret and with the Turret

Room. Answering my 'Good morning' with an 'Aye, it's no a bad day,' followed by a keen look from her grey eyes, the old body paused as though about to say more. That was unusual, and I waited expectantly. Then apparently she changed her mind, and with the tantalizing remark: 'I'm hearing Black Dougal will be back then,' she went on her way. Who 'Black Dougal' was, she left to my imagination, and I knew it would be useless to question her. Doubtless she regarded 'Black Dougal' as her own – like Cairntoul itself – and, if he were a ghost, then she was unwilling to share her ghost with other intruders who were of the solid flesh. Not unnaturally I connected him with my visitor; and, from the way Mother Lum had spoken, I gathered that to the initiated he was by no means unknown.

For a week or two nothing disturbed the even tenor of our way. Then, unexpectedly, came a message from the War Office to say that a Mr Mowat was on his way to fill the vacancy in my team. And at once the problem arose: where should we sleep him? If I were to suggest his sharing a room with one of the others when my old room stood empty, then perforce I would have to tell my tale. In the end I decided to stick to the old excuse: the Turret Room was a poor room, frightfully draughty, with a 'howl' from the outside grille whenever the wind blew in a certain direction, and so forth and so on.

But I had reckoned without our new recruit. When he arrived, alert and confident, nothing I could say would persuade him to 'double-up' with one of the others. There was an empty room. He had slept in far worse places than a room with a draught and a howl. He was insistent. I was halting. And, in the presence of the others, pride kept me from telling the truth.

Mowat went up to the empty room, while I made a mental reservation that I would tell him about my 'visitor' as soon as I could get him alone. But although, later, I was to see him alone more than once, by then my story had paled before his own experience.

He had arrived late in the afternoon, and again it was twilight. Stupidly, I had been so intent on persuading him not to take over the Turret Room that I had failed to connect both *time* and *place*. And only when there came a strangled cry from above, did I curse myself for forgetting that upon both occasions my 'visitor' had come with the dusk.

We raced to the stair and to the Room. Bursting open the door, we found Mowat lying on the floor in front of the table, almost exactly as I had been found in my 'faint'. He was lying on his back, with his arms spread-eagled; but it was his face that caused us to cry out. Even in the dim light we could see that it was suffused with blood, while his eyes seemed to be sightlessly staring at us with a look in which agony and terror were horribly combined.

Sanderson, who had taken a medical degree, and who was our 'doctor', was quickly on his knees and moving professional hands over that still body.

Mercifully, Mowat was not dead, and that same night we got him into a nursing-home in Aberdeen. But it was a full three months before he was out again, when, upon my own urgent recommendation, he was posted to Southampton and given the task of coping with the many problems raised by officers coming on leave or returning overseas. I had to think of some post where he would be kept too busy to remember Cairntoul; and the R.T.O.'s office at Southampton had always seemed to me to be about the busiest of its kind.

But I am going much too fast. Long before Mowat was out of the nursing-home it had become one of my major tasks to try to induce him to tell his tale. It was clear that if only he could unburden himself, his recovery, and particularly his recovery in mind, would not be long delayed. But the terror had bitten deep, and I daren't tell my own tale first, lest, instead of encouraging him, I should only increase the torture of his mind. At long last, however, I induced him to speak, and the tale, when it came, was much the same as mine. There was this difference, however: Mowat, terrified and powerless, even as I had felt powerless, had seen the face in the mirror; he had seen it slowly draw nearer, the hate in its eyes seeming to burn into his soul; he had felt the hands at his throat; and then, suddenly, those hands had tightened into a grip, powerful, relentless and *strangling*. With that, he thought he gave a cry before unconsciousness intervened. 'But what was "it"?' he asked me. 'And how did "it" get in?'

I noticed his use of the word 'it'. So he also had doubted the nature of his visitor. But the only answer I could give him was to tell him of my own experience, to ask him to forgive me for allowing him to use the room, and, above all, to assure him that he had finished with Cairntoul for good.

After that unburdening, Mowat recovered quickly, and, as I have said, he was posted direct to Southampton, far removed from the Province of Mar. Meantime, at the castle, we sedulously avoided the Room, but also we took one positive action. We smashed that mirror to fragments and, having carefully collected the fragments, we threw them into an enormous fire, specially built-up for the occasion, where we watched them melt and fuse. Later we collected the shapeless glass nodules and, with the ashes, buried them deep in the earth. Later still, I had one further brief passage with Mother Lum, but her pronouncement, far from being helpful, only increased the mystery.

I had come back from visiting Mowat in Aberdeen. Meeting her outside the iron yett, I said cheerfully: 'Well, Mr Mowat seems to be progressing famously now.'

'Mowat, did ye say?' she cried with a wild look in her eyes. 'A Mowat is it? May heaven save him!' And with that she hobbled away.

'Heaven has,' I muttered, somewhat irreverently, as I cast innumerable though silent maledictions on her retreating figure.

And that, as you can see, took me no further.

Then, early in June 1940, the War Office suddenly decided to disband my team. We left Cairntoul and, in the urgency of new tasks, the mystery of Black Dougal and the Turret Room gradually lost its hold and became a bad memory and little more.

With the end of Hitler and the surrender of Japan, I returned here to the humdrum labours of my Anthropology Department; and yet it was here, in the academic peace of the University, that I learned what had previously been denied.

I had been back perhaps a week or ten days when Henderson, of the History Department, asked me if I would give a lecture to his 'mediaeval' students. Naturally I agreed, and, during the course of the conversation, I happened to mention that I had been stationed for a while at Cairntoul in Mar.

'Did you see the ghost of Black Dougal?' he asked.

I pride myself that I didn't start.

'Why?' I said. 'Is the castle haunted?'

'It's supposed to be,' he answered, cautiously, 'and with one of the best authenticated ghosts we have. There's quite a story behind it.'

And, to conclude, the story I got from Henderson was roughly this:

Some time about the middle of the sixteenth century, when the Mowats of Cairntoul and the local branch of the Camerons had been long at feud, an attempt was made to end the feud by a Mowat-Cameron marriage. So Mowat of Cairntoul married the daughter of Cameron, but, after a week or so, when the Camerons had gone home, Mowat brutally strangled his wife and then sent defiance to the Camerons.

I should add that Mowat was supposed to be mad, but naturally the Camerons were paying no attention to that. They turned out to a man, and, Cairntoul being what I have already described to you, they were wiped out to a man, and nary a footing did they get on that staircase. Wiped out to a man, yes; but there was a young brother to the murdered bride – a boy, Dougal, then about six years old. And upon Dougal fell the whole burden of a new and a more bitter feud. As he grew up, the boy, and then the man, nursed his revenge – and so came the name 'Black Dougal', from the hate that burned in his eyes.

But there was little chance for Black Dougal in the Mowat country, unless he went there by night; and by night the mad Mowat sat and laughed in the Turret Room where he had strangled his bride. Yet mightn't that give Black Dougal his chance? One night, in the gathering dusk, and the manner of it no one knows, Dougal made that impossible climb up the castle wall, right up to the beacon-turret, only to be beaten at the end by the overhang of the turret's corbelling. Struggling to breast the corbelling he fell – a sheer forty feet at least – and was killed outright.

At that Mad Mowat only laughed the louder. But, within a week, he had caused an iron grille to be made to enclose the open turret at its top. Within another week, he was found dead in the Room – strangled, as there he had strangled his bride.

———— ·◦§⟡◦· ————

'And now you know why never again will I look into a mirror at twilight,' continued Drummond, after a pause. 'Yet there is one further point which makes it all more puzzling still. I'm convinced that no one could climb that outer wall to the beacon-turret. Yet one of our signallers, an honest, sober, and thoroughly unimaginative fellow, had other views.

'It appears that about the time when we were rushing upstairs, after hearing Mowat's strangled cry, this signaller was walking back to the castle after making some adjustment to the aerial in the old dovecot. Happening to look up to the turret, he was astounded to see a man hanging there by his hands. Then, to his horror, the man dropped like a stone.

'For a second our signaller stood still. Then he ran forward as fast as he could. But, to his astonishment, the climber, who should have been killed outright, picked himself up, ran round the corner of the castle, and out into the open country beyond.

'With a shout (which, of course, in our own preoccupation we didn't hear) the signaller went in pursuit. Doggedly, in the gathering darkness, he followed his man. Before long, he could see him only against the light in the sky. The man came to a small hill, breasted it, stood silhouetted for a moment on the top, and then disappeared down the other side. In turn our signaller breasted the hill but, when he came to the top, his quarry was nowhere to be seen.

'Admittedly it was dark; and admittedly a man might easily take cover in a fold of the ground. *But later I was to discover that the Cameron country started on the far side of that hill.*'

The Eve of St Botulph

The Eve of St Botulph

I HAD BEEN lecturing to my class on chronicles and annals, and I had called their attention to a memorandum in the Chronicle of Melrose recording the loan of certain folios of that chronicle to the Abbey of Dundrennan. Thereafter I had spoken of 'borrowings' and of 'common sources', and I had even tried a mild joke by referring to Max Beerbohm's comment that, whether or not history repeated itself, historians certainly repeated one another. With the conclusion of the hour the class had dispersed, and I was making my way across the quadrangle to the University Library when I was intercepted by one of the students:

'May I ask a question, sir? We know that Dundrennan borrowed almost the whole of the Chronicle of Melrose. Did it borrow to read, or to copy? Was there a Chronicle of Dundrennan?'

'We don't know of one,' I answered briefly, excusing myself, for I was particularly anxious to look up an article by Ferguson in the *Scottish Historical Review*, and to take some notes from it, before attending one of those tiresome committees which, under present dispensations, absorb far too much of the teacher's time.

But I was destined to 'cut' my committee and to learn, for the first time, that there *had* been a Chronicle of Dundrennan; more than that, I was destined to learn not only of its discovery, but also of its subsequent mysterious loss.

I had just started on Ferguson's article, and I had already noted two wild assertions wholly unsupported by the evidence, when Mair, our Librarian, interrupted me.

'I thought you'd like to see this,' he said, putting a folded packet of papers in front of me.

'What is it?' I asked, casting a hasty glance at the packet. Then I looked more closely, and my mind took in what had caught my eye. Written in a neat hand on the outside of the packet were the words: 'To be opened in the event of my failure to return. Alexander Hutton.'

'However did this come into the library?' I continued, pushing aside my *Scottish Historical Review*. 'And who was Alexander Hutton?'

'Oh! Alexander Hutton's all right,' answered Mair, easily. 'He was a minor antiquary of the early nineteenth century. As for the packet, I found it among General Donaldson's papers. He too was a minor antiquary of about the same time, and all his books and papers were presented to us after his death. Actually I was looking for a description of the Cross Kirk at Peebles, which I knew was in amongst his papers, when I came across this.'

'Have you read it?' I queried.

'No,' replied Mair. 'I haven't even opened it. I'll admit I was strongly tempted to open it, especially after reading that super-scription, but then I thought that perhaps I should bring it before the Library Committee. However, you are on the Committee. What do you think? There would surely be no harm in opening it. Hutton must have been dead for at least a hundred years.'

'No harm at all,' I answered quickly. 'Clearly Hutton won't return now, so, equally clearly, we are justified in obeying his injunction.' And with that I took up a paper-knife, broke the seal, and carefully unfolded the packet.

There were four sheets of paper covered with writing in the same neat hand.

Mair sat down beside me and together we began to read:

Kirkcudbright

If this is read by eyes other than mine it will mean that I have died as strange a death as can come to any man. It is my intention, when I return, to burn this document as being simply an account of a foolish fantasy. But there is always the possibility – strange as it may seem – that I may not return from my adventure. Accordingly I leave this record. If it is to be read by others, it must be interpreted by them as best they may.

First, however, I must give some account of how I come to be in Kirkcudbright.

I had long been of opinion that the Abbey of Dundrennan had kept its own chronicle. To give my reasons would be irrelevant to my present purpose and would take too long. Moreover, if I return from my projected adventure, my arguments will be developed elsewhere. Suffice it to say that when, about a month ago, General Donaldson wrote to me, announcing the discovery of an early manuscript chronicle in the attic of an old house here in Kirkcudbright, I knew that my opinion would be proved correct. And so it was. For three days I have barely left my room in this inn; for three days I have been closeted with a manuscript which is none other than the original codex of the Chronicle of Dundrennan.

At first General Donaldson would have had me stay with him; and I would have been glad to accept his hospitality. But his wife, I knew, had been failing for some time, and the General himself, now nearly ninety, was far from enjoying his former robust health. I knew this excellent inn well; I had stayed here before; here I could stay again.

'Well, stay at the inn, if you must,' General Donaldson had said. 'And take the manuscript there. You can then carry it off to Edinburgh for as long as you may want to borrow it. But if you are to stay for more than a day or two – to get what our romantic writers now call "atmosphere" – we shall hope you will find time to dine with us at least once before you leave.'

'Atmosphere'! That word is now much in my mind as I write; and should it happen that this is to be read by others, they will well appreciate the reasons why.

For two whole days I was fully and happily occupied with my manuscript. But now all that has changed, and I am disturbed and distracted. For to-day, for the first time, I have examined those three strange passages. Today I have paid a visit to the north grange of the Abbey, and there 'imagined' things. Tonight I shall visit the north grange again, 'on the eve of St Botulph'.

Writing these events in their proper order, I must record that this morning, on opening the manuscript of the Chronicle, I noticed on one of the early folios (the twenty-first folio, verso, to be exact) something that I had previously overlooked. There, following an account of affairs in Galloway, I noticed for the first time that the immediately following four lines had been expunged and, in their place, had been inserted a brief list of the reigns of the Scottish Kings from Malcolm II to Alexander II. Before, I had paid no attention to that uninteresting list of kings; in fact, I had skipped it. But now, noticing for the first time that it had been overwritten, I was naturally curious to know what had been so carefully expunged. Try as I would, however, the most I could make of the original entry ran, in translation:

on the eve of St Botulph ....
.... a lay-brother ....
saw .... the north .... abbot
.... devil .... prayers ....

Then, remembering that I had also skipped other and somewhat similar lists, I ran my eye hastily down the next folio and there, under the entries for the following year, again I saw a list (this time a list of the Popes, and their dates, from Urban II to Innocent IV) again covering an expunged passage, and this time one which had run to no less than eight full lines. Once more I strove to decipher the original entry; and this time, owing to the way in which the later scribe had been compelled to spread out his list of Popes, I was much more successful. This time, in translation, the entry ran:

> on the eve of St Botulph the same lay-brother when returning to the north grange by the way that traverses the wood was spoken to by a stranger of soft step and dark habit who for a space accompanied him .... candle .... die by fire .... by many signs and words .... escaped with difficulty .... entered the grange and there .... Telling this to the abbot .... for the second time .... devil .... by prayers

Wondering vaguely what all this could mean, I glanced quickly down the page, and then overleaf, looking for a similar entry for the following year. And there it was! This time the list was one of the dates of the foundations of the Cistercian houses in Scotland and their first abbots, and the expunged passage was much shorter. This third entry, moreover, had been too carefully expunged and the inserted list of houses and dates and abbots was too full. All that I could decipher was:

> on the eve of St Botulph the ....
> same lay-brother ....
> .... by fire ....
> .... that same night

But I also noticed that the two immediately following lines, which had *not* been expunged, had no initial capital letter, and, being in the hand of the original entry, had apparently formed its conclusion. And those two immediately following lines ran:

> the north grange of the abbey was burned
> and in it the lay-brother lost his life

then some expunged words which appeared to have been: *May God receive him in the celestial choir*, and for which the later scribe had substituted: *through the badly fixing of a candle*.

Once more, and with eager curiosity, I looked through the entries for the following years, but no further lists had been inserted. No further passages had been expunged. The tale, such as it had been, was ended.

For a time I tried to puzzle out the story of this unfortunate lay-brother, his encounter with the Devil, and his death in the burning of the northern grange. Pulling out a sheet of paper, I wrote down the entries as I have given them here. Clearly on the first occasion, on the eve of St Botulph, the unhappy lay-brother thought he had been approached by the Devil, and, seeking the help of the abbot, had apparently been counselled to prayers. On the second occasion, again on the eve of St Botulph, the dark stranger, the Devil, had openly accosted the lay-brother, had probably tempted him, and had accompanied his temptation with a threat of death by fire. Again the abbot had apparently replied that the Evil One could be overcome only by prayer. Finally, next year, the lay-brother *had* died by fire in the destruction of the north grange. He had died the death that had been threatened; but whether or not he had met the dark stranger for a third time before his death was not recorded. His death that same night had prevented any account of his closing day.

So much for the expunged passages. But why had they been expunged? It seemed more than likely that a later abbot had deemed those entries unfit for the Abbey's Chronicle. The north grange had caught fire, and the lay-brother therein had lost his life, through carelessness in the fixing of a candle. That, and no more. The Chronicle had been purged of a record that would assign too great a power to the Prince of Darkness.

Then, moved solely by a scholar's curiosity, I turned up a list of Saints' days. The feast of St Botulph fell on the 17th of June. And today was the 16th! Tonight would be the eve of St Botulph and the anniversary of the adventure of the lay-brother of Dundrennan.

At first I was tempted to walk over to General Donaldson's house and to share my discovery with him. Then came a sudden desire to keep my discovery to myself. It was about eleven o'clock in the morning. I determined to walk over to the Abbey lands forthwith and to try to find the ruins of the northern grange. Then, perhaps, if I felt bold enough, I would again visit the grange when evening fell – I would visit the grange on the eve of St Botulph *to see if any dark stranger would accompany me.*

Fortunately, I had already borrowed from General Donaldson's library all his local histories and all works containing drawings and plans of Dundrennan. I had soon located the north grange, and, between it and the Abbey, 'the wood'. Taking my stick, I at once set forth. I had left the town and was on my way to the Abbey a little before noon.

The 'wood' had disappeared – though I could mark its site – and the north grange, when I had found it, was little more than the foundations of one wall. The ground was thick-grown with nettles, and, at some early period, an attempt had been made to enclose the ruins of the grange with a ring of large standing stones. One of these attracted me. Rubbing off the lichen with my hand, I saw what had caught my eye. On one of its sides the stone bore a roughly-incised cross! Did the other stones bear a like sign? Breaking down the nettles with my stick, I moved quickly from stone to stone. On three stones out of every four I found the same incised cross, sometimes distinct, sometimes almost undecipherable through the weathering of the stone. Clearly at one time *all* the stones had been so incised; and on all the stones the crosses were on the side *away from* the ruins. Was there here some concept of a sacred ring that would enclose the Evil One and imprison him? Had this encircling ring, marked with the cross, and doubtless fortified in other ways, been raised after the destruction of the grange and the death of the lay-brother who had perished here and whose end was not unconnected with the visit of some evil spirit?

Whether I was influenced by my discovery, and these thoughts that followed it, I cannot say. But I now noticed that whenever I was within the area bounded by the stones, I felt a strange feeling of oppression, much like that which one feels on a sultry summer afternoon just before the breaking of a thunderstorm. Also, though again it was probably only some absurd fancy, I had the impression that as I moved about, sometimes within the ring of stones, sometimes outwith the ring, not only did the atmosphere change, but even the light also. Whenever I was within the ring the day seemed to grow darker; outwith the ring, the day grew lighter again.

I believe I spoke aloud, damning myself for a fool. And then I noticed the stranger! He was dressed in a dark suit or surcoat, and he was standing in the place where I had located the site of the 'wood'. To say that I was unaffected by his appearance would be untrue. Certainly I felt my heart beating more quickly and a strange sudden breathlessness come over me. I put my hand on to one of the incised stones to steady myself from falling. Then, recovering, I rubbed my eyes. The stranger had gone! Again damning myself for an imaginative fool, I left the ruins of the grange and began to make my way back here to the inn. Passing the site of the 'wood' I noticed nothing unusual, and I sensed nothing unusual. An hour later I was back in this room.

For perhaps half-an-hour after my return I debated with myself whether I really *had* seen a 'stranger of dark habit', and whether I really *had* sensed a different atmosphere within that enclosing ring of incised stones. Had I not imagined it all from my deciphering of those expunged entries in the Chronicle? And if there *had* been a 'stranger', was it not likely that he was some local farmer curious to know why I was examining the ruined grange? But within that half-hour I had made up my mind. At half-past five by the clock I began to write this full account of my discovery in the Chronicle of Dundrennan and of my visit to the north grange in the broad daylight of a summer's afternoon. I have made it as detailed as I could. I have now finished it, and I shall seal it and leave it on the mantel-shelf of my room where it will be found in case anything untoward should happen to me. For I am determined to find out whether or not I was guilty this afternoon of a foolish fancy. I have determined to find out whether or not, after the lapse of nearly six hundred years, the 'dark stranger' will still accost and accompany one who walks to the north grange by the way that traverses the wood. On the eve of St Botulph I shall take that walk myself.

ALEXANDER HUTTON
16th June, 1825

Mair and I looked at one another.

'And that's that,' I said non-committally.

'But he can't have returned,' put in Mair. 'If he had returned, he would have written another account to take the place of this one. And why did no one open it? Unless it's all a hoax?'

'No, it's not a hoax,' I answered slowly. 'It rings too true for that. As you say, he can't have returned. What then happened to him? Does the date help?'

Again we looked at the document.

'The 16th of June 1825,' murmured Mair. 'I wonder if . . .'

'Yes,' I interrupted. 'We could try what newspapers there were. There may be something.'

Mair went off at once to collect all the local newspapers which the library possessed for the year 1825, and impatiently I awaited his return. At last he came. Nor did he return empty-handed. The riches of the library were revealed. Mair was accompanied by a boy pushing a trolley with some ten or twelve bound volumes of early newspapers.

Together we tackled the volumes, and it was not long before I heard Mair give an exclamation. I went over to join him. It was the *Wigtown Advertiser* for 18th June 1825; and there Mair had spotted:

GENERAL DONALDSON

We regret to inform our readers of the death of General Donaldson, a gallant soldier and a noted antiquary. The General died very suddenly at his house about midday yesterday, the 17th. He had been in indifferent health for some time and was known to have been much affected by the strange accident in which his friend and fellow antiquary, Dr Alexander Hutton, lost his life. We are informed that the General had only just returned from a visit to the inn in Kirkcudbright where Dr Hutton had been staying, and that he had made his way to his library on an upper floor in the house, when he was heard to fall. The servant who rushed into the room found the General lying on the floor, but, on lifting him up, realized that his master was dead.

Thereafter followed details of the General's career, both national and local – but those details were not for us.

'Strange accident in which his friend and fellow antiquary, Dr Alexander Hutton, lost his life,' repeated Mair.

'Yes, we're getting hot,' I answered. '*And*, if General Donaldson carried Alexander Hutton's document home – and the people at the inn would be more than likely to give it to him, as Hutton's friend; and, remember, it bore a mighty strange superscription that would certainly make them look askance at it – would not the General take it to his library to open it and read it? Assuming it fell out of his hand when he collapsed, it is just possible that the servant picked it up from the floor and placed it, without looking at it, among other papers on the library table, where, perhaps, it became mixed up with them and eventually, unnoticed and unknown, found its way here to the University Library with all the rest of the old man's papers. Just possible. At any rate, that would be one explanation why it has remained unopened until today. But let's see if we can discover what the "strange accident" was.'

But apparently the *Wigtown Advertiser* was too concerned with General Donaldson, or knew too little of the way in which Alexander Hutton had lost his life. The *Wigtown Advertiser* yielded nothing more.

Once more we tackled the bound volumes on the trolley and this time it fell to me to find the report for which we looked. The *Stewartry Record* filled the gap:

STRANGE FIRE IN KIRKCUDBRIGHT

During the night of the 16th June a strange fire occurred in one of the rooms of the 'Douglas Arms' in Kirkcudbright, resulting in the death of its occupant, a visitor, Dr Alexander Hutton.

Dr Hutton had been out for a walk in the evening and had returned to the inn, apparently in some haste, and somewhat perturbed, about 11 o'clock. He went straight to his room – when, shortly afterwards, sounds were heard as though he were in great agony. The door was lock-fast, but, being broken open, one corner of the room was found to be burning furiously and, in the middle of the flames, lay the prostrate body of Dr Hutton. The fire was extinguished with some difficulty – though those who fought the flames were unable to understand what could be burning so furiously in the one part of the room where there was only a desk and a chair. It was also noticed that the rest of the room, including that part where the fireplace was, but without a fire, was wholly untouched by the blaze.

Dr Hutton was found to be dead, though again it was difficult to account for his death as his body, despite the fact that it had seemed to be in the very centre of the flames, bore no marks of burning. The desk and chair, however, were completely burned; and it is thought that the fire may have started on the desk, among the papers accumulated there. It was also noticed that Dr Hutton had not turned up his lamp, which was lit, burning only on a low wick, and which was standing in that part of the room untouched by the fire. Here another strange aspect of the affair was noted, namely that, although the lamp was lit, Dr Hutton must have been using a candle at his desk – for a melted portion of a candle, wholly unlike the ones in use at the inn, was found near the burned-out desk.

It is thought possible that the lighted candle may have been insecurely placed on the desk, and, falling over, may have been the cause of the fire.

———··········———

Since this was written we learn that a valuable manuscript which Dr Hutton had borrowed from General Donaldson is missing. This manuscript was probably on the burned-out desk, and, if so, must have been completely destroyed. We also learn of a strange story that Dr Hutton was not alone in his room. Mr James Kennedy, who had been at the house of his daughter (she having just given birth to a son), was returning to his own house about 11 o'clock when he saw a man, whom he believes to have been Dr Hutton, making his way towards the 'Douglas Arms'. His attention was particularly drawn to this man, not merely because he was running towards the inn, but also because of the way he seemed to stagger as he ran and occasionally even to stumble, much as though he had run a great distance and was completely exhausted. But Mr Kennedy, when watching the running man, was convinced that he saw a second man, dressed in dark clothes, following closely behind Dr Hutton (if it was he), but following so easily and quietly that at first Mr Kennedy wondered whether he was not being deceived by some odd trick of the light, and whether the 'second man' was not simply a strange shadow. This sense of a shadow, more than of a second man, was emphasised when Mr Kennedy saw the dark shadow, or man, follow Dr Hutton through the door of the inn. When the door was opened by Dr Hutton, the two figures seemed to pass into the inn at one and the same time.

Unfortunately, Mr Kennedy's story is without confirmation. Although the people of the inn heard Dr Hutton rush upstairs to his room, stumbling more than once on his way, no one was heard to follow him. And, shortly afterwards, when Dr Hutton's cries were heard, and when the door of his room was broken open, he alone was found in the room, lying in the midst of the flames, as already described.

I saw Mair's shoulders give a sudden jerk, as though he were trying to rid himself of an unwelcome burden.

'Horrible,' he muttered, almost to himself. 'And Satan answered and said: "From going to and fro in the earth, and from walking up and down in it."'

Can These Stones Speak?

Can These Stones Speak?

WE HAD GATHERED round the fire in the Smoking Room of the University Club. Outside it was a raw wet day with a laggard fog, and there was every inducement to linger in the enjoyment of an easy-chair, a cheerful fire, and the pleasure of good company. Moreover, the talk had turned to the interesting subject of coincidence.

'In my own case,' said Robertson, taking up the talk, 'the queerest coincidence I can remember came with a telephone call. I had left the Mathematical Institute fairly early, intending to come here to read the papers before lunch. By pure chance I had turned eastwards in Chambers Street, so that my way took me by the more roundabout route over the North Bridge and along Princes Street, and there, again by pure chance, I suddenly decided to drop into Purves's to buy myself a new pipe.

'Almost as soon as I had entered the shop, however, one of the assistants came up to me to say that I was wanted on the telephone. Now that, you'll admit, was strange; for no one knew of my sudden impulse to buy a pipe. How then could I be wanted on the telephone?

'Well, to be brief, I went to the telephone at the back of the shop, only to find that the call *was* for me and (and here is the queerest part of it all) the call had come through to Purves's, instead of to the Mathematical Institute, by some strange failure in the working of the automatic exchange.'

Robertson paused impressively. 'And I should say,' he continued, even more impressively, 'that in Edinburgh the mathematical chances of being given a wrong number by an automatic exchange, and a particular wrong number, just at the time when a particular individual is present to answer the call at that particular wrong number, must be, let me see . . .'

'Yes, yes,' put in several of us at once, for Robertson's informal lectures on the theory of probability were well known. 'An extraordinary coincidence! The chances against it happening must be enormous.'

'And yet,' came the quiet voice of Henderson, our mediaeval historian, 'I can tell you of an even stranger coincidence – if that is the right word – and one also connected with a call on the telephone, but one which I think even Robertson will admit is beyond all reckoning.'

———·•·———

As you know, began Henderson, the University Court of one of our sister universities has long made a practice of purchasing old and historic houses within the town which, after careful restoration and the sympathetic addition of modern conveniences, it makes available as residences for the members of its staff. Thus the University, in addition to acting as an energetic Ancient Monuments Board for the town, also exercises a maternal care for its supposts and provides them with lovely and interesting houses at rents within the reach of an academic purse. And in one of these lovely old houses (called *The Monal* – and the name was later to prove significant) lived my good friend, Alexander Lindsay, the University Librarian.

At the time the Lindsays moved into their new, or perhaps

I should say their old, house I had been making regular visits to the University Library in order to transcribe one of its manuscripts; and I well remember the excitement with which I was shown over *The Monal* and asked to admire its fine ceilings and fireplaces, the thickness of its outer walls, the sweep of the staircase, and (at the special prompting of Mrs Lindsay) the splendid way in which the domestic quarters had been rearranged, and a bathroom and a cloakroom installed.

'And isn't it haunted?' I asked, playfully.

'Well, if it is, we haven't noticed it yet,' was Lindsay's laughing reply.

The manuscript upon which I had been working (and this is not wholly unconnected with my tale) was a local account of local affairs at the time of the Reformation. It was an excellent account and, to my mind, almost as valuable as the well-known *Diurnal of Occurrents*. It contained, for example, a detailed description of the skirmishing between the army of the Congregation and the French forces of the Queen Regent; and it had a graphic relation of a visit, and a sermon, by John Knox, followed by the 'purging' of the local 'monuments of idolatry'. But, as it happened, the Lindsays had moved into *The Monal* just about the time when my transcript was coming to an end, and, because of that, I was out of touch with them for about a year.

Then came Lindsay's letter – reproaching me for not having visited them, reporting an interesting manuscript discovery, and making a strangely guarded offer of hospitality for any week-end I might choose. Lindsay, it appeared, had been making a new catalogue of the manuscripts in the University Library, and had discovered several folios of a Burgh Court record which fell within the period of my own particular manuscript but which, having been bound up with a lawyer's collection of styles and statutes, had hitherto escaped notice. 'There are one or two entries which will interest you almost as much as they interested us,' ran his letter; and then came a sentence like this: 'We will gladly put you up for any week-end next month, though I should warn you that we can offer only the "pillared room", and this house, it appears, is not without its ghost, and a ghost, moreover, that can now be identified.'

Naturally I replied at once, accepting their kind invitation (with some light remarks about the ghost), and a fortnight later – on a Friday night in June – I was making my way towards *The Monal* through the cobbled streets and narrow wynds of the town.

The Lindsays were delighted I had been able to come and, after the usual greetings, Lindsay himself escorted me to my room. I looked round it with interest but, to my casual glance, the 'pillared room' revealed nothing unusual apart from two massive stone piers complete with their capitals, which had been built into one of the walls and which were clearly of much earlier date than the house itself.

'So this is the haunted room?' I said.

'Yes,' he replied. 'But I'll tell you about it later. There's a meal waiting for you downstairs, so don't spend too much time knocking on the walls or looking for secret passages. The bathroom is just across the landing.' And with that he was gone.

During dinner neither the room nor the ghost was mentioned and, after coffee, Lindsay at once invited me into his study to look at the newly discovered burgh records.

'Here's the manuscript,' he said, handing to me a heavy quarto. 'I'll confess I've broken every library rule by bringing it here, but you'll find the burgh records at the very end – the last ten folios.'

I took the volume eagerly and, turning to the end, found there a number of folios in a typical clerk's hand of the second half of the sixteenth century and with the usual rubrics of a burgh court:

Curia burgi de S. tenia ibidem in pretorio ejusdem per Alexan-drum Bannerman et Johannem Blar ballivos dicti burgi . . .

'The most interesting entries are those under the dates 17th November 1573 and 20th April 1574,' he continued.

It did not take me long to find the first entry to which Lindsay referred, and at once I realized the reason for his own interest in this record of the past. Couched in the legal phraseology of the time, I read that the Nunnery, which had been 'unoccupeit sen it was last purgeit', was now 'much decayit and abil hastilie to fall doun', and that therefore the provost, bailies, dean of guild and town council had given permission to Andro Black, mason, to 'tak the stanes thairof' at the 'sicht of the dene of gild' for the 'bigging' of a house on a piece of land 'boundit' ... and thereafter followed the 'gate' and the boundaries of the land to east and to west.

I looked up and caught Lindsay's eye.

'That's your house, all right,' I said. 'The boundaries are quite definite. That is, if Andrew Black did take the stones and build.'

'Oh, he took the stones, right enough,' Lindsay answered, 'and he built. Hence *The Monal*, in which you can now recognize the Latin *moniale*, or nunnery. But read the other entry, for 20th April 1574, and then you'll see why we have a ghost.'

Quickly I turned the leaves to the entry for 20th April 1574. But this time the passage I was meant to read lay not in the formal record of the sitting of the court, but in a scribbled memorandum made by the clerk at the foot of the page. And there, in a couple of lines, the clerk had noted that 'intimation' was to be made to the minister anent the bones found by Andro Black between the north wall of the Nunnery and two of the pillars there.

'You see what that implies?' queried Lindsay.

'You mean that Black had come across the remains of a nun who had been immured?'

'I'm afraid so. For although part of the north wall and some of the piers are still standing in the ruins of the Nunnery, it would appear that Black did not hesitate to use part of the wall and those two pillars. In fact he seems to have used them for one of the walls of your room, and the stones and piers he used must have been those where the remains were found. The bones of an immured nun never troubled that thrifty builder. But they seem to have troubled our last two visitors, both of whom slept in your room.'

'Queer sounds?' I asked.

'Yes. Nothing serious. Just a faint insistent knocking that defies identification and that gradually grows fainter and fainter until it dies away.'

'Well, that doesn't sound too bad,' I replied. 'And I'm quite ready to sleep in your "pillared room". A ghostly tapping will be a new experience, and especially so now that I know the whole history of the knocking ghost.'

'Good,' answered Lindsay. 'I had an idea you would be interested; though naturally I thought it best to word my letter as carefully as I could.'

We left the study and joined Mrs Lindsay in a small drawing-room that overlooked a long restful garden similar, I thought, to that of the house in St Andrews where the ill-fated Mary Stewart was said to have drawn her own bow in an archery contest with one of the douce citizens. As we entered, Mrs Lindsay said the one word: 'Well?'

'Well it is,' I replied. 'Your spectre seems to be no more than a knocking on the wall; and I'm ready to listen to most things once.'

'That's all right then,' she answered. 'But neither Sandy nor I could be absolutely sure. And although this seems a big house, actually the "pillared room" is the only room we can offer to our guests.'

Our talk drifted to other topics, and for a while the 'pillared room' was 'clean forgot'. But about half-past eleven, when I rose to retire for the night, Mrs Lindsay gave me a quick, questioning glance.

'It's all right,' I assured her. 'Tomorrow you shall have my own version of the knocking nun.'

———————·•✿•·———————

As I slowly undressed, I wandered round my 'pillared room' examining its walls, and aimlessly testing here and there the panelling or stone. For when the house had been taken over and restored by the University, the plaster had been stripped from the walls and replaced by some lovely old panelling which ran all round the room, save on the one side where the two piers with the stone wall between them stood uncovered and bare. 'Strange,' I remember murmuring to myself, 'it almost looks as if the workmen themselves knew the story of the nun immured.' And with that, I climbed into my bed, switched off the bedside lamp and, untroubled by midnight fancies, was soon fast asleep.

What first awakened me I cannot say. Indeed I cannot say whether I was awake, or whether all that followed was merely a dream. All I can tell you is that, awake or dreaming, I heard *the noise*. To call it a knocking would be misleading. Rather it was a steady scrape and tap-tap exactly similar to the sounds a blind man would hear were he to stand by a bricklayer at work. And the pauses were the same – the same scrape of the mortar gathered up, the same tap-tap on the brick to seat it firmly in its place, and then the same scrape of the trowel to remove the mortar from the outer face of the wall. So it went on: scrape, tap-tap, scrape. But brick by brick? No! With a sudden surge of horror I realized that I was listening stone by stone to the immurement of the nun; listening to a grim entombment of the living flesh, conjured up from some dark shades beyond the fathoming of man. And as that harrowing noise went on I felt my nerves beginning to give way. That inexorable scrape, tap-tap, scrape, which meant so much and yet which left so much more to be imagined, was too horrible to be endured.

Then, just when my nerves seemed stretched too far, a bell began to ring, sharp and shrill. Strangely enough, the new and wholly different sound seemed to bring immediate relief: partly, perhaps, because it took my mind from that other and more awful sound; partly, perhaps, because I realized that although the bell was ringing somewhere in the house, it was not ringing within my room. Urged by some impulse that it is impossible to explain, I slipped out of bed, made for my bedroom door, opened it, and felt my way on to the dark landing outside. The bell was ringing downstairs – strident, persistent, demanding immediate answer. And suddenly, all at once, I realized it was the telephone. The telephone and nothing more. But, instead of the normal double-ring and pause, the bell was ringing continuously as though its summons were too urgent to allow for any intermission.

Moving as quickly as I could in an unfamiliar house, I descended the stairs and felt for the table on which I had noticed the telephone when I first arrived. I took up the receiver and at once the ringing ceased. Bending down, I said: 'Yes? This is Dr Lindsay's house.'

But through that instrument came no normal and reassuring voice. Instead there came the sound of a voice, far distant or strangely muffled, intoning some phrases in measured and sonorous Latin. Then came recognition! I was listening to the concluding dread sentences of an excommunication: 'And as this candle is now extinguished so may her light be extinguished before Him who liveth for ever and ever. May her soul be sunk in the nethermost pit of Hell ever there to remain. So be it. So be it. Amen.'

Again so much was heard but so much more was left to be imagined. Nor did the horror end there. For, as my mind took in that awful scene, there came through Lindsay's telephone a sound such as that which might be made by many candles dashed to the ground and so extinguished, followed at once by the slow tolling of a bell, deep-toned and relentless.

Had I really *heard* that grim echo from the past? Had those sounds really come to me through the telephone in my hand? Fumbling to replace the receiver in the dark, I dropped it on the table, and there I let it lie. I stood trembling, my lips still repeating the closing sentences of the excommunication, my ears still ringing with the tolling of the bell. I turned, and struggled painfully back upstairs, only to halt, with renewed fear, as I reached the threshold of my room. Suddenly, I felt cold, bitterly cold, and I realized that I was shivering from head to foot. I must get back into my bed at any cost! With something between a stumble and a rush I reached my bed and hastened to draw the blankets round me – and perhaps over me! But somehow they seemed perverse and obstinate, and I was shivering more violently than ever. I sat upright in my bed and strove to gather the sheets and blankets into some sort of order. And then I felt the wind! It was blowing hard outside, almost a full gale, and strong gusts of wind were beating upon me from the open window. I was certainly awake. Awake, and sitting up in bed; holding the blankets in front of me, and shivering with cold.

Had I dreamed it all? Time to think over that later. Quickly I slipped out of bed and across the room to shut the window. And there was *the noise* again! Scrape, tap-tap, scrape. For a second I stood paralysed. But now came an overwhelming surge of relief. The scraping noise came from the window – the catch was giving slightly to and fro with each gust of wind; and the tap-tap came from something loose outside, something that was tapping against the window, likewise with every gust of wind. So *that* explained it all! I shut the window and went back to my bed, calling myself every kind of fool. But just before a refreshing dreamless sleep intervened I remember asking myself: 'But what of that telephone call? How does *that* fit in?'

Henderson leaned back in his chair, and the tension relaxed. Yet before any of us could speak he continued:

'I said there was a coincidence, however; and here it is.

'We were having breakfast next morning and I had just finished the story of my dream.

'"How horrible!" exclaimed Mrs Lindsay. "What an awful night!"

'"Not a nice dream, by any means," added Lindsay. "Yet it fits in with all the usual theories. We had been discussing the immurement of the nun and Andrew Black's use of the piers and the stones. It only needed the scrape of the window-catch and that tapping noise – and there's your dream."

'"All of it?" I asked quietly.

'"Why? . . . What? . . . What do you mean?" asked Lindsay.

'"I suppose it's only an adjunct to the dream," I answered, "but somehow or other I can't fit in that telephone call. Why should I dream that? The continuous ringing of the telephone bell, instead of the usual short double-ring and pause; the concluding sentences of the excommunication; and then the extinction of the candles and the tolling of the bell. There could be no association of ideas there. We had not mentioned excommunication, and the thought of excommunication had never occurred to me."

'A slight cry escaped Mrs Lindsay, and she put her hand up to her mouth.

'"Why, my dear . . ." began Lindsay.

'"I've just remembered," she said, almost in a whisper, and with a startled look in her eyes. "When I came in to prepare the breakfast this morning, I noticed the telephone-receiver was lying on the table, and I replaced it. I wondered then who had left it like that. But *in your dream*," she continued, turning to me, "you fumbled with the receiver, you dropped it on the table, *and you left* it there!"

'And as the three of us sat at the breakfast table, each battling with the impossibility of every strange surmise, a bell rang, sharp and shrill.

'I think we all jumped, involuntarily. But it was only the bell of the front door. The bell rang again. Mrs Lindsay rose to answer it, and, as she left the room, she left the door ajar. We heard her open the front door, and we heard a voice:

'"Good morning, ma'am. I'm from the Post Office. Your telephone wire is down. Came down in the night with the wind. But we'll soon connect you again. The men are on the job now, though there's a fair stretch of it to be repaired."

'There was a murmured reply from Mrs Lindsay. Then the voice began again:

'"No! It won't be a big job. But it's queer the way it came down. You won't believe it, ma'am, but the wire from your house was blown clean off its course; right across the ruins of the old Nunnery; and queerer still, it was coiled there so tightly round one of the old pillars by the north wall that we had quite a job to get it free again."

'I looked at Lindsay, and our eyes met. *Trailing across the ruins of the old Nunnery, coiled round one of the piers so tightly that it could hardly be released.*

'"And that's the explanation of your tapping noise," said Lindsay, striving to sound as matter-of-fact as he could. "I wondered what could be loose outside your window. And of course it was the telephone wire. It's connected to that corner of the house."

'I didn't answer, and I had a shrewd suspicion that Lindsay didn't expect me to.

'Then, literally, I could see him pulling himself together. "And I suppose a broken wire like that might easily lead to some kind of short-circuit which would give a continuous ring. That's possible, isn't it?"

'Still I didn't answer him, and still he persisted. "Yes, it all fits in now. Just a dream, my friend, just a dream. A damned bad one, I'll admit. And this business of the wire stretching across the ruins of the old Nunnery, and tightly coiled round one of the remaining columns there, is simply a strange coincidence. Coincidence and nothing more. After all, haven't we all rather jumped to conclusions about those bones found by old Andrew Black? There's nothing to prove they were the remains of an immured nun. And would a sentence of excommunication be pronounced before or during an immurement? More than that, is there a single recorded instance in Scotland of the immurement of a nun?"'

Again Henderson moved in his chair.

'I didn't answer him,' he continued. 'I didn't ask him how he would explain that telephone-receiver which Mrs Lindsay had found still lying on the table. I didn't ask him if that also was a coincidence. More than that, I'm certain he was relieved that I didn't ask. Perhaps there are some questions it is better not to ask. Perhaps there are some experiences into which we should not inquire too closely. And perhaps because of that, I have never sought to know whether a sentence of excommunication *would* be pronounced at the time of the immurement of a nun.'

The Work of Evil

The Work of Evil

EVER SINCE HIS return to duty from his long illness, Maitland Allan, our Keeper of Printed Books, had been singularly reluctant to grant any access to the Special Collections which were in his charge; so much so that the Rare Book Room in the Library had become well-nigh as sacred and as difficult to enter as the secret courts of an Eastern harem. Thus, when he suddenly said to me: 'Come, and I'll show you the whole Collection,' I was taken completely by surprise.

I had asked for an early Italian work by Aeneas Sylvius.[2] The assistant at the library counter had disappeared with my form. Allan had come back with him. And now, strangely, I was to be shown 'the whole Collection'. Was this simply a piece of unexpected good fortune? Or had the old man some ulterior purpose? I had noticed during the last two or three weeks that he had made a point of stopping to talk to me whenever we met in a room or corridor. Had he singled me out in some way from the rest of my colleagues? And if so, why? Everyone knew that his recent illness had made him a little 'queer'.

Opening a door marked 'Staff Only', Allan led the way through a maze of book-lined passages until at last, passing a heavy steel door, we stopped before an inner iron grille. This he unlocked and, stepping aside, he ushered me into the room.

I glanced around with curiosity; but he gave me time for no more than a quick glance.

'There they are,' he said, pointing to one of the stacks. 'An extraordinary collection. A frightening collection. The *Lucretia and Eurialus* which you want happens to be in it, but it's very much of a stranger there. For the rest, I hate them,' and his voice rose nervously as if in emphasis.

I walked over to the stack, but I noticed he did not accompany me. There, as I saw two long rows of beautiful bindings, I murmured something of my appreciation and delight. Reverently taking down one volume after another, I examined the bindings more closely. All were of rich leather elaborately tooled in a variety of intricate patterns in which whorls and strange cabalistic signs predominated. I also turned to the title-pages: every work was either an *incunabulum*[3] or of a date early in the sixteenth century. But every work was on the same theme. I ran my eye along the shelves, picking out the volumes which bore titles on their spines. Still the same theme.

'Why!' I exclaimed, turning towards him; 'they are all on black magic and necromancy. What you might call a collection of evil; or at any rate a collection of evil intent. Who on earth gathered together all this devilry? It looks as though someone was striving hard to find something which at last would work.'

'An unfortunate young man whose history you know as well as I do,' answered Allan, slowly. 'John, third Earl of Gowrie. You may remember that after studying here he became a law student at Padua, and was there said to have dabbled in magic and witchcraft. Well, here's his library – or part of it. And I wish it had never survived.'

Again I noticed the nervous pitch in his voice.

'Well,' I replied, lightly, 'if he did dabble in the forbidden art he must have found it pretty ineffective. The very number of his books shows that. One would have thought that constant experiment followed by constant failure and disappointment would have been bound to bring disillusion.'

For a full minute Allan made no reply. Instead, he gazed at me with an odd look in his eyes.

'"Ineffective"!' he said, at last. 'I wish to God you were right! Do you see that safe over there? It contains one further book belonging to Gowrie's collection. No one knows it is there but myself – and now you. That book is the one book which, at last, Gowrie found *would* work. Listen to me – you *must* listen to me – and I'll tell you a tale of devilry that has tormented me ever since this collection came in. Then you'll believe in "effectiveness".'

He had pointed to a small safe in a corner of the room. I made a step towards it, but he seized me by the arm.

'Often I feel I must take the book in that safe and throw it into the middle of the sea,' he continued, 'but I can't do it. I'm too afraid. Only one small book, yet it is evil itself. That one book seizes a man by the throat and strangles him to death.'

I looked at him in astonishment. Could it be Allan who was saying all this, and who was holding my arm so tightly that his fingers were biting into my flesh?

'Whatever do you mean?' I asked, partly disturbed, and partly angry at being held as though I were a child faced with something which might be dangerous.

'I wish I knew,' he replied slowly, and in a quieter tone. 'All I can tell you is that within the last eighteen months two men have been strangled to death after looking into that book. That's all.'

I was dumbstruck. And not without reason. We stood there, tense and silent, like two conspirators surprised by something they couldn't name and fearful of what it might mean.

The Collection came to us towards the end of the war, said Allan, breaking the silence at last. It came from the local Antiquarian Society, and it came in the wooden boxes in which it had been stored when Gowrie House was pulled down in 1805 and in which it had remained, untouched, until we opened those boxes in this very room nearly one hundred and fifty years later. It is said that the books were discovered in a wall closet which had been panelled in and so lost to sight. It may well be so. Perhaps Gowrie himself entombed them that way. Perhaps he, too, tried to rid himself of an evil incubus. Perhaps Gowrie put one particular book, with all its fellows, into a hidden closet, as I have put that one particular book into a safe. Perhaps he, too, was afraid to do the one thing he ought to have done. Or perhaps he did something else. Perhaps he put his own curse upon the book that no one should again open its pages and live. That, at any rate, has been its history here.

First it was Fraser, who, you will remember, was our Professor of Chemistry before you came. As soon as the Collection arrived he was all agog to see it. Day after day he was here with his note-book. 'Working out their formulæ,' he would say to me. 'Damned interesting, some of them.'

But one day he read too much. I had been in the Reid Room that afternoon, and I didn't come here until nearly closing time. Fraser, as usual, was in his seat by the window there; but, that afternoon, he didn't look up with his usual cheery nod. Instead, as he looked up at my entrance, I saw that his face was drawn and white. 'My God, Allan,' he said in a strained voice, 'this book is the Devil himself. It should be burned. Burned to ashes.' He pushed his chair back and seemed to recover himself. 'Look,' he continued, glaring at me with fierce earnestness, 'I'm putting it here, in this empty case. Lock it in. And let no one, no one, ever read it again.'

He strode to that wire-fronted case over there – it was empty then – thrust in the book, and waited for me to lock the door with my master key. Then he pushed past me and went out. It was the last I saw of him.

That same night he was found dead in his own room in the lab. Strangled. And no one could explain how or why.

He had a queer kind of lab-coat of which he was very proud. It was like an old-fashioned smock which was tied by a fancy cord running through the neck. When he was found, his hands were gripping that cord. It had been drawn so tight that it had throttled him. The students working in the lab had seen no one go into his room or come out of it. I know now that they *wouldn't* see anyone. I know, too, that Fraser's hands were at that cord in a vain struggle to loosen it, and live.

No one thought of connecting Fraser's death with the book he had been reading. At first I hardly associated the two events myself. Yet it was not long before I found I was growing frightened of that book, lying by itself in its locked case. I tried to avoid looking at it, but it seemed to force its presence upon me. Perhaps a fortnight passed before I realized the truth. Then, suddenly, I knew. I knew that Fraser's death had been caused by it.

Frightened as I was, I still had courage enough to do one thing. Unknown to the rest of the staff, I removed from the library catalogue all the entries relating to it. Fraser's death should not go unheeded. No one should read that book again. No one should even know of its existence. Had I dared, I would have burned it – as Fraser had said it should be burned. But I couldn't bring myself to touch it. Already it had me in its power. I was afraid of it. And so young Inglis had to die. A second victim.

He had come to us as a part-time student assistant, and had quickly proved his worth. So much so that special tasks were soon assigned to him automatically. And, at a time when I was unluckily absent for a few days with influenza, he was given the task of checking the shelf catalogue of the Special Collections. You can imagine my horror when, on the day of my return to duty, I found him here, holding *the book* in his hands, open, and reading it.

As soon as he saw me he called out: 'I've found an *incunabulum* which is not in the catalogue. It's filthy with dust . . .'

But I rushed up and seized the thing from him. I shoved it back into the case and relocked the door, while he looked at me open-mouthed. But what could I say? I simply dare not tell him the truth. As I saw it, to tell him the truth would be to tell him his own sentence of death. I made some feeble excuse, which I know he didn't believe, and sent him off. Then I sat down, sick and faint. What could I do to save him? Nothing. He was doomed. The evil thing was upon him, and he could never escape. I cursed myself for my own cowardice. Why, at least, had I not warned him? Had the book so laid its spell upon me that I even feared the ridicule which might follow my warning?

Poor beggar. He didn't escape. When the library was closing that night, one of the staff found that the automatic lift wouldn't work. Naturally he assumed that someone, on one of the floors, had failed to shut the door properly; and he went to look. He found the door which wasn't shut. He also found Inglis. He was trapped by the outer door, and, strangely, he was trapped by the neck. Almost as though he had entered the lift and then, as the door was sliding-to, had put out his head to look at something. Stranger still, but only to those who didn't know what I knew, the poor fellow was dead. I tell you, the pressure of the outer doors on that lift is so light that you can hold them back easily with one hand. Yet Inglis was dead. He had been throttled by the light pressure of a lift-door. Fraser had been strangled on the day he had opened the book. So had Inglis.

Can you wonder that the same night I had what was called a nervous breakdown?

I was away for over a year and, as you probably know, I have only been back for some six weeks or so. Surprisingly, I have kept my reason – though sometimes I'm not sure. Perhaps I am mad;

or perhaps I am suffering from some delusion. Yet I was the only person who knew that Inglis had opened the book; I was the only person who knew that Inglis was doomed to die. And he did die. As Fraser had died.

God forgive me! I should destroy the thing. But I daren't. I am too afraid of it. Yet about a fortnight ago, the day I spoke to you in the Upper Hall, I was brave enough to move it out of the bookcase and to lock it away in that safe. You gave me the courage to do that – even though you didn't know you had done so. Now, I am afraid again. I feel it is laughing at me behind that steel door . . . and biding its time.

You *must* forgive me; but I *had* to tell you all this. One day I, too, may be found strangled. And you, at least, will know the reason why.

As you may imagine, I was not particularly pleased at having this extraordinary burden of knowledge so suddenly thrust upon me. Yet, as I crossed the Quad back to my own room, my thoughts ran in a different vein. 'Poor old Allan,' I thought. 'No wonder he had a breakdown. No wonder he is "queer". Fancy living with *that* on your mind all the time. Poor wretch! A victim to his own imagination: with a harmless book locked up in his safe, and fearing it as though it possessed all the malignant power of some genie in the *Arabian Nights*. And mortally afraid to do the one thing which would bring relief.'

But I did Allan an injustice.

I had given my lecture next morning, and was talking to a student in my retiring-room, when Wallace, one of the lecturers in the Modern Languages Department, and Allan's next-door neighbour, opened the door and beckoned me outside.

'Did you know Maitland Allan was dead?' he asked.

'Dead?' I repeated.

'Yes. Apparently last night he was all worked up about something. Kept walking up and down his study, saying in a loud voice: "I *will* do it. I *will* do it"; and generally worrying his housekeeper out of her wits. Then, suddenly, about nine o'clock, she heard him go into the hall. Peeping round her door she saw him put on a cap, his scarf and his overcoat, and literally rush out of the house.

'By this time thoroughly alarmed, she came to us. I did my best to calm her down, but she was so upset that in the end I offered to go back with her and to wait up with her for Allan's return.

'He didn't come in until nearly two o'clock in the morning. We heard him open the front door and then, just when he had shut it again, we heard him give a queer kind of strangled, choking cry. We rushed into the hall and saw him half-hanging from the door and half-sprawled on the rug in the hall. One end of his scarf had caught in the door as he had shut it and, when he had turned away, it had pulled tight round his neck and had trapped him. We opened the door at once and released him, but, when we tried to help him to his feet again, we discovered to our horror that he was dead . . . I came over to tell you for I believe he had taken quite a liking to you . . .'

But I was no longer listening. My thoughts were rushing madly towards one word which seemed to loom larger and larger. And the one word was 'strangled'. Fraser; Inglis; Allan. Could it *all* be coincidence? Or could such things indeed be true?

Naturally the Procurator Fiscal conducted an inquiry into Allan's death.

A boatman stated that Allan (whom he identified) had knocked him up about midnight and had asked to be rowed 'a full mile out to sea'. At first he had demurred, for Allan had seemed 'fair demented'; but an offer of five pounds had seemingly settled the matter. He had rowed Allan out to sea and, when he had told him that they were well beyond the full mile for which he had asked, Allan, to his utter surprise, had suddenly plucked a small book from his coat pocket, had raised it with both hands above his head, and had hurled it down into the water with all his force. Then, said the boatman, 'he crouched him down in the boat as though he were afraid someone was going to hit him. And he stayed like that till I tied up again, when he jumped out of the boat and fair ran along the quay as if the Devil himself was chasing him.'

The doctors were puzzled, but unanimous. Despite the softness and natural elasticity of the scarf, they had been surprised to find a sharp mark around Allan's neck. But they were convinced he had died of shock. His heart, they said, was in poor condition; any shock would probably be too much for it.

And I alone knew what that 'shock' would be. I alone knew what would flash through the poor wretch's mind when he felt that sudden, unexpected tightening of his scarf around his neck.

So much I had written yesterday when my mind was free. But how different is today! Today all Allan's fear and dread are now my own. Today, at the close of the Library Committee, our Librarian spoke casually, as of a matter of little importance. He had looked over the Rare Book Room, he said, after Allan's death, and there he had found, inside the safe, a book that belonged to the Gowrie Collection but which, to his surprise, *had no entry in the catalogue.*

Dazed and bewildered, I have found my way back to my room. And, as I write this down, I am a prey to every wild imagining. Can it be that Allan, deranged and overwrought on that last fearful night, cast the wrong book away? How could he? It was the only book within the safe. Yet reason recoils from that other thought – that a book can return from the depths of the sea. Reason? How long can reason prevail against this fearful question that is now pulsing through my mind? Already our Librarian has handled the book, and opened it.

The Return of the Native

The Return of the Native

'THE TROUBLE WITH all you Scots is that you live too much in the past.'

Galbraith was trailing his coat as usual, but this time it was MacDonald, our visiting Fulbright Professor, who took up the challenge.

'The trouble is that sometimes we cannot escape the past,' he said.

'None of us can,' retorted Galbraith. 'The past in the present is obvious all the time.'

'I meant something a little different from that,' replied MacDonald. 'I meant a past that may come back, unexpectedly, to disturb the present.'

For once Galbraith seemed to be at a loss. 'In what way?' he asked, lamely.

'Well,' answered MacDonald. 'I could give you one instance from my own experience, if you'd care for it. It's a story I don't often tell, and I can't say that I emerged with credit; but it certainly underlines the point I wanted to make.'

Our American guest looked at us a little shyly, as though wondering whether he had broken one of the rules of the Common Room in offering to recount a 'personal experience'.

He was quickly reassured: and this was his story of a past which could not be escaped.

———·⟡·———

About a year after the end of World War II, when I was still an officer in the American Intelligence, and stationed in London, I decided to seize the opportunity of visiting Scotland and seeing, for the first time, the land of my folk. I had little difficulty in obtaining a fortnight's leave and, after spending a week-end in Edinburgh, I hired a small car to drive to Arisaig and Morar – the district from which I knew my forbears had emigrated some two hundred years ago.

Setting off from Edinburgh on the Monday morning, I made that marvellous drive through Callander, Lochearnhead, and Tyndrum, and on through Glencoe to Ballachulish, where I put up for the night. Passing through Balquhidder country on my way from Callander to Tyndrum, I had recalled the story of assembled Macgregors swearing their oaths on the severed head of a royal forester; and, as I had passed through Glencoe, I had recalled the tragedy of sleeping MacDonalds who were massacred by those to whom they had given food and shelter. Yet that night, in the inn at Ballachulish, as I brooded over the stories of the past, I little thought that I myself was soon to be touched by the past – touched too closely for my liking – and simply because I, too, was a Mac-Donald, though a MacDonald of a different sept from the MacIans of Glencoe.

The Tuesday morning broke fine and clear. Leaving Ballachulish, I crossed by the ferry and took the lovely road by the shores of Loch Linnhe and Loch Eil, and on to Glenfinnan, where Prince Charlie's standard was raised, and where I thought the monument a poor thing to commemorate so stirring an event. From Glenfinnan the scenery became more wonderful still, as the narrow road, still 'unimproved', twisted and turned on its ledge between the hills and the sea: and I remembered I was on 'The Road to the Isles'.

It may be that my head was too full of the tales of the Young Chevalier, or it may be that my eyes strayed too often to the beauty of land and sea: I do not know. But, almost too late, I caught sight of an enormous boulder crashing down the hillside and almost on top of my car. Braking hard, and wrenching the wheel violently to the right, I lost control of the car and ran into the bank of the hill, while the boulder, missing the front of the car by inches, thundered across the road and bounded over the opposite verge.

Slightly shaken, I got out to see what damage I had done, and, as I did so, I was astonished to see an old woman standing on the other side of the road just where the boulder had crashed across. For a moment I wondered how she had escaped; then, something in her appearance made me look at her more closely. I was startled to see that her dark and deep-set eyes were glaring at me with a look of intense hate. I saw, too, that water was dripping from her clothes and that her grey hair was hanging round her shoulders, dank and wet. And, looking at her, I experienced a strange sense of danger, or it might even have been fear, which it is wholly impossible to describe.

So we stood, facing one another, and myself in a kind of trance, until, suddenly, the woman turned away and, apparently stepping down from the road, disappeared over the edge. Recovering my wits, I ran across the road, only to pull myself up with a jerk. On that side of the road, and guarded only by a single strand of wire, there was a sheer drop of a hundred feet or more to the rocks on the loch-side below. Had I wrenched my wheel the other way, or had that boulder crashed into my small car, broadside on, nothing could have saved me.

I made myself look again at that sheer drop. What had happened to the old woman? There was no sign of her anywhere. Not even a ghastly huddle of body and clothes on the rocks below. Yet I had seen her clearly enough; and she had stepped down from the road at this very spot. And why had she glared at me with such bitter hate? Surely I had not fallen asleep at the wheel and dreamed the whole thing – a boulder crashing down and a malevolent old hag with dripping clothes?

I walked slowly back to the car, trying to puzzle things out. Fortunately the car was not badly damaged: a buckled wing and little more. But it was firmly wedged in the bank and would not move. I sat down beside it and waited for help. And help soon came in the shape of a delivery van; its driver fortunately had a length of rope; and within a few minutes he had hauled me clear.

'You were lucky in your skid,' he said, cheerfully. 'Had you skidded the other way you'd have finished driving for good. And it would have been pretty difficult to recover your remains for the funeral. However, all's well now. And that front wheel seems all right, too. But it's queer the way you managed to skid on a dry surface like this.'

'I didn't skid,' I replied, slowly. 'I was trying to avoid a boulder that was rolling down the hillside on to the road.'

'Boulder!' he answered, looking me hard in the eye. 'It's the first time I've heard of a boulder rolling down on to this road. And I've driven over it six days a week for the last twelve years or so.' Then, still looking me straight in the eye, he wavered a little and condescended to add: 'However, strange things do happen. But I'd like to know where that boulder came from. So long.'

He waved a friendly hand, got into his van, and drove off, leaving me alone with uncomfortable thoughts. I was positive I had not fallen asleep. I was equally positive that a large boulder had missed my car by inches. And what of that old woman with her dank hair and dripping clothes, who might almost have risen from the waters of the loch below, and who, after glaring at me with burning hate, had apparently been swallowed up in the waters again? If not, where had she gone? And who was she, anyway? How did she fit in? 'Well,' I said to myself, resignedly, 'strange things certainly do happen. But I'd be glad of an explanation, if anyone could give it.'

I stepped into my car, started the engine, and drove on again. Possibly I was more shaken than I had at first realized, and possibly I was worried with my thoughts; certainly I now crawled along the road, through Arisaig, and on to Morar. I remember that when at last I pulled into the drive of my hotel I felt as though a great burden had suddenly been lifted from my back.

———————

Morar is a lovely spot, with its stretch of silver sand and with the islands of Rum, Eigg and Muck standing like sentinels in the sea. Inland, I found delightful walks, especially one by the side of the loch. In a couple of days the old woman of my adventure on the road from Glenfinnan had become a puzzling memory, and nothing more.

I had reached Morar on the Tuesday evening. Wednesday and Thursday I spent in lazily wandering about, or in lying in the heather and feeling how good, for a time, was a life of ease. On Friday, much against my inclination, I caught up with some long-delayed mail from home and then, in the early evening, took a short walk that led to the falls, where the waters of the loch, at that time still unharnessed for electric power, poured through a gorge before finding their way to the sea.

I had scrambled down a steep and narrow path that led to the foot of the falls, and had taken my stance on a boulder there, when a noise, rising above the thunder of the falls, made me turn round. I was only half-interested, and I turned round casually, but, to my horror, I saw a large rock hurtling down the narrow path on which I stood. How I managed to make the right decision in a split second of time, I shall never know. I flung myself down behind the boulder on which I was standing. The rock struck it with a mighty crack, bounced harmlessly over my head, and plunged into the whirlpool at the bottom of the falls.

Dazed and trembling, I carefully picked myself up. Then

pain made itself felt, and I discovered that I had injured my left knee by throwing myself down to the ground. Would I be able to climb back again to the top of the path? I looked up at that steep and broken slope, and my heart suddenly jumped into my throat. An old woman with dank grey hair, and with clothes that were dripping wet, was glaring at me from above; glaring at me with intense hate, as three days before she had glared at me on the road from Glenfinnan. And again, though this time far more pronounced, I felt the same strange fear, and, with it, a weakness that seemed to affect every part of me.

I gripped the boulder beside me with both hands, frightened lest I should fall backwards into the whirlpool below. Gradually the weakness passed. Then, summoning the little courage that was left in me, I began a slow and painful crawl on hands and knees, taking advantage of every turn in the path, and praying constantly that no other rock would be hurled against me from above. When, at long last, I reached the top of the path, I lay there completely exhausted and unable to take a further step. The old woman was nowhere to be seen.

As I lay there, worn out and riddled with fear, my mind strove vainly to grapple with accidents that were beyond all reasoning. I now knew definitely that I had not fallen asleep at the wheel of my car. I knew, too, that twice a fiend of an old woman had tried to send me to the shades from which I was convinced she herself had risen. I had had enough. If, all unwittingly, I had disturbed the haunts of some avenging 'ghost', the only answer was to leave her haunts forthwith. Call me a coward, if you like; and coward I certainly became! But, then and there, I determined to return to Edinburgh and the safety of its streets.

I limped slowly back to the hotel, intending to pack my bags and depart. Yet, as soon as I had reached the hotel, a new fear struck me. To leave forthwith would mean driving through Arisaig, and on to Glenfinnan, by night. I couldn't face it. I knew that even driving along that road by day I should be crawling at a snail's pace, and looking to the right and the left of me all the time. I even had thoughts of driving the odd four miles into Mallaig and there putting myself and my car on the boat. In the end I decided to stay the night, and to leave on the Saturday morning.

After dinner I told the landlord of my decision to leave early the next morning. I excused myself by reference to some urgent business that had arisen from my mail; and, in expressing my appreciation of the comfort of my stay, murmured something of my regret at having to leave so soon, and before I had even made any attempt to trace my ancestors who had come from Morar about two hundred years ago.

'Have you seen Father MacWilliam?' came his unexpected reply.

'No,' I answered. 'Why do you ask?'

'Well, it will be this way,' he said. 'The Father knows the history of Morar. He's been at the books and the papers these many years. And he's the one who would be telling you about your own folks, way past, if, indeed, there is anything to be known of them at all.'

'Could I call upon him now?' I asked eagerly.

'Indeed you could; but he'd be out.'

I looked at him in surprise.

'He'd be out, for he's in my own parlour this very time. Come you with me, and you can have a talk with him before you go.'

Full of interest, I was led to the back-parlour of the hotel, where Father MacWilliam, a plump and rosy-faced priest, was snugly ensconced in an easy-chair, and deep in the pages of an enormous book.

'Father, I've brought you Mr John MacDonald,' said my host, without further ado. 'He's for leaving tomorrow, but he'd be glad if you could be telling him of his people who, it would seem, came from these parts maybe two hundred years ago. If I were to let the two of you talk together, maybe he'll be learning something of what he wants to know.'

The priest gave me a warm smile of welcome, and somehow managed to unfold himself out of his chair. The landlord gave us a nod, and left the two of us together.

'John MacDonald,' said the priest, looking at me. 'It tells me nothing. Everyone here is a MacDonald. Every man, woman and child. God bless them all. Could you tell me more?'

I had to confess that I couldn't. All I knew was that my forbears had left Morar, or some place in its vicinity, about the 1750s. That, and no more.

Father MacWilliam shook his head. ''Tis no use,' he said. 'I can be of no help to you, much as I would have liked. Too many MacDonalds have left these parts – and sometimes I think too many have stayed on. But there, you've had a good time for the few days you've been here. And that's aye something.'

'Yes,' I answered slowly, and then, with a sudden desire to unburden myself, 'a good enough time if it hadn't been for an old woman who has twice tried to stone me to death.'

'What?' shouted the priest, his eyes suddenly blazing. 'You will be telling me that! Were her clothes dripping with water? Did you see, man, did you see?'

'Yes,' I answered, quickly. 'They were dripping wet. And she glared at me with such hatred in her eyes that I knew she was trying to kill me. Who is she? Or what is she?'

'I know only too well what she is,' he replied, slowly and quietly. 'And I know now who you are, John MacDonald, and I can give you your forbears. I'm thinking, 'tis well you'll be leaving when the morning comes. But tell me your tale, and I'll tell you mine.'

Briefly I told him of my two encounters – on the road from Glenfinnan, and on the path by the falls. I told him, too, of the feeling of fear that had come to me. 'But why,' I protested, 'why should this old hag – ghost or spirit or fiend or whatever she is – hate me, a complete stranger, and try to murder me?'

'Because you are no stranger,' answered the priest, gravely. 'You are a MacDonald of Grianan, and the curse is on you and all your kin. That's why. And there's more to it. The same curse made your own people sell all, pack up, and sail across the seas in the year 1754. And though I'd be the last man to be frightening you, I shall be glad when you're back in your own land again.'

'But the thing's impossible,' I burst out, even though my own experiences had told me the very contrary.

'Not at all,' he replied firmly. 'Doesn't the Holy Book itself speak of evil and foul spirits? And didn't an evil spirit attack the seven sons of Sceva, leaping upon them, and driving them away, wounded and naked?'

'Well, what is the curse?' I demanded impatiently.

'That the stones of the earth shall crush you and all your kin,' answered the priest, looking at me sadly. 'And I'd be glad to be seeing you escape.'

'But why should there be such a curse?' I pleaded.

'Listen, my son. Away back in the seventeenth century the MacDonalds of Grianan were big folk, holding their land by charter of the king and with a right of judging the people on their land – even with a right of *furca et fossa*, a right of "gallows and pit", a gallows for hanging guilty men, and a pit for drowning guilty women. And in that time, when many a poor woman was put to death because she was reputed to be a witch, Angus MacDonald of Grianan, you'll forgive me, was a cruel man. Then it was that Isabel Mackenzie, a poor creature on his lands, was accused of witchcraft because a neighbour's cow had sickened and died. Isabel Mackenzie was condemned to death, and Angus MacDonald, the cruel man, decreed it should be death by drowning. Did not his own charter say so? That poor creature was tied by her wrists to the length of a rope; the rope was tied to a boat; and Angus himself, with others of his house, rowed out into the loch, dragging her behind them till at last she was drowned.

'Then, it is said, as the waters slowly ended her unhappy life, she cursed Angus and all his kin. "The waters of the loch shall drown me, but the stones of the earth shall crush you and all your kin – *Pronnaidh clachan na talmhainn thu 's do chinneadh uile.*"'

The priest paused. 'And so it has been,' he continued, with a sigh. 'Angus laughed, as the years passed and he still lived. But one night, in a storm of wind, the chimney of his house was blown down and the stones of it fell through the roof and crushed him to death where he lay in his bed.

'Alastair, his son, was of finer mould. I can find no word of him doing wrong to man or beast. Yet he, too, was to die. There was a jetty to be built – and this was maybe a full twenty years after his father had died – and Alastair had gone down to see the men at the work. There was a tackle of some kind for lifting the heavy stones, and, somehow, a stone slipped from the tackle. It fell on him and crushed him to death.

'Then it was that people began to look at Grianan and quietly, among themselves, began to talk of the curse. And then it was that the MacDonalds of Grianan began to die more quickly. Always there was a stone of the earth in the way of their dying; and some of them, with their last words, would be speaking strange things – of a woman with burning eyes, and whose clothes were wet with the waters of the loch. And, in the end, one, Roderick MacDonald, having seen his own father crushed to death by a millstone that was firmly fixed and yet somehow broke loose, sold his lands and his cattle, and sailed to America with his wife and child.

'And you, my son,' said Father MacWilliam, laying his hand gently on my arm, 'you are come of Roderick's stock. Yet I see some comfort for you. In all the papers that I have read, Isabel Mackenzie's curse never failed before. Twice it has failed to touch you. To me it would seem that her evil power is on the wane. I shall pray for you. But I shall still be glad to see you gone.'

'And I can do nothing?' I asked lamely.

'Nothing, save to put your trust in God,' he answered. 'And to remember that the power of the Lord is greater than all the powers of evil.'

Again he touched me lightly on the arm, looked kindly at me, and went out.

———·•⁝⁚·———

To be quite frank, I do not remember very clearly how I passed the rest of that evening. I was already completely unnerved, and now the story of my own house, the house that had the curse upon it, occupied my mind to the exclusion of all else. I wanted company. I wanted to have people around me. And yet my mind was never on the talk that they made. I am ashamed to think how boorish and uncivil I must have seemed. I am ashamed, too, to think of the drink that I took. I freely admit that terror had taken hold of me. Terror of being left alone. Terror of going to my bed. I drank in the bar, trying to make friends with complete strangers and yet thinking always of an old woman and her curse on my kin. In the end, I am told, I had to be carried to bed by the local doctor and a guest at the hotel. For a time, drink had ousted terror.

I do not know what time it was when I awoke. It was already daylight – but daylight breaks early in the Highlands in summer time. My head ached violently. Then I remembered my heavy drinking, and, with that, I remembered its cause. But what had awakened me? The wind was blowing strongly and yet, I assured myself, not strongly enough to bring a chimney-stack crashing down. But what was that? My ears caught a strange noise that seemed to come from the corridor outside my room. At once all my terror returned. I sat up in bed. There was the noise again!

A shuffling noise. And something more. A noise that came between each shuffle. What was it? A shuffle; a strange dull thump; a shuffle; a thump. And drawing nearer all the time.

I tried to shout, but I could only croak like a feeble frog. I jumped out of bed, trembling from head to foot. How could I escape? Outside, in the corridor, a hell-hag, dead three hundred years ago, was coming to me, coming to crush me to death with a stone. A stone! That was the noise I could hear! She was pushing it before her, pushing it up to my door!

I looked wildly round. Thank God! The window! Flinging it wide open, I climbed quickly out, and, hanging from the window-ledge by my hands, let myself drop. As I landed on the ground I fell over backwards and, at that same instant, there came a heavy thud at my feet and the soft garden-earth splashed over me. I lay there, paralysed with fear.

Then, slowly, I raised my head to look. A large stone had embedded itself in the ground exactly where I had dropped and exactly where I would have been had I not fallen over on my back. The curse was still upon me, and my life was to end with a stone.

I sprang to my feet, and, strangely, found my voice again. With a wild cry I ran across the garden, my injured knee sending quivers of hot pain up my thigh. And immediately I was held in a fast grip. Trembling and overwrought, I whimpered like a beaten cur, only to be at once calmed and reassured. I had run straight into the arms of Father MacWilliam.

'You are safe, my son,' came his gentle voice, as he still held me in his arms. 'Safe and saved. The powers of darkness shall trouble you no more. I have wrestled, even as Jacob wrestled at Peniel. Come with me to my own house. The Lord forgive me: I should have taken you there before.'

Paying no attention to the confused hubbub that now came from the hotel, he led me gently across the road – its stones feeling smooth and cool to my bare feet – and over the open moorland to the church. There he took me into his house and put me in his own bed. On the instant, I fell into peaceful sleep.

Late the next morning I awoke to find my clothes on a chair by my bed. I washed and dressed, and went downstairs. A wise and gentle priest was awaiting me. He gave me breakfast, and then took me to my car which, with all my luggage packed and neatly stowed on the rear seat, was standing at his gate. 'There you are, my son,' he said. 'The curse is at an end. You can take any road and drive on it as freely as you wish – though,' he added, with a twinkle in his eye, 'always observing the laws that are enforced by the police.' He gave me his blessing, and wished me God-speed. With unashamed tears in my eyes, I thanked him again and again. At last I drove away.

Without a qualm, without fear of any kind, I drove back through Arisaig and Glenfinnan, back through Ballachulish and Callander, and so to Edinburgh.

——— ·•҉•· ———

Yet my tale has not quite ended.

On my way back, I stopped at Ballachulish for a very late lunch at the inn. As I ate alone in the dining-room, I heard two men talking outside by the open window.

'That was a mighty queer business last night, though I could get nothing out of the landlord when I tried to pump him this morning.'

'Yes, but the fellow was obviously drunk. He had to be carried to bed, you know.'

'I agree, old man. All the same, there was more to it than that. As you know, my room was next to his, and, just before he gave that awful yell which woke up everybody, I'd already been wakened by a strange kind of bumping noise which I couldn't fathom. I got up and looked out of the window, thinking the noise was probably coming from outside – and it may well have been that coping-stone, which had obviously worked loose, and which the wind may have been lifting slightly before it fell.

'However, that's not what I was going to say. As I looked out of the window, there, in the clear light of the early morning, I was astonished to see the local priest standing in the middle of the lawn, with one arm raised above his head, while a dishevelled old woman crouched and cowered before him. The very next second I saw this fellow climb out of his window and drop down. There was a crash as the coping-stone fell. And, with that, he jumped up, gave his appalling yell, and rushed straight into the arms of the priest. Where the old woman had gone to I don't know. She just seemed to disappear. And what she and the priest were doing . . .'

'What an extraordinary . . . Did you . . .'

The men had moved away, and their voices were fading. I tiptoed as fast as I could to the window and strained my ears. But I could catch only a few more words.

'And another queer thing – when I dashed out into the corridor in my bare feet it seemed to be soaking wet all along its length.'

Quieta Non Movere

Quieta Non Movere

I HAD JOINED a group in the Common Room and found Staunton holding forth on Black Andie's 'Tale of Tod Lapraik'.[4]

'That solan "pyking at the line",' he said, turning to Patterson, 'is the finest touch in the whole tale. It's part and parcel with the eerie nature of the Bass Rock itself.'

Patterson nodded. But it was Henderson, our mediaeval historian, who spoke next.

'Yes,' he said, slowly. 'I agree with Black Andie – and Staunton – that the Bass is an "unco place". "Eerie", as you say. But there's another place, not so very far from the Bass, where there is also "the plash of the sea and the rock echoes", but which, to my mind, is more eerie and more awe-inspiring still. I mean the ruins of Wolf's Crag,[5] on that precipitous and well-nigh inaccessible promontory of rock, with the cliffs rising sheer behind them. And while Stevenson could write a tale to fit the Bass, Wolf's Crag, as you know, has its own tale – that queer story about Barbara Napier and the black dog. It, too, is a story which fits the very place itself, which could almost be a part of it, and which can be said to be even stranger than "Tod Lapraik", for some of it is true and can be checked from contemporary records and accounts.'

'Don't know it,' said Staunton, bluntly. And when it was soon evident that we were all equally ignorant, Henderson told the following story that is now haunting my mind to the exclusion of everything else – and for reasons that may sound fantastic but to me are only too real.

One or two of you – Aitken, I expect, for one – will know that in 1594 Logan of Restalrig, who then held the castle of Wolf's Crag, made a formal agreement with Napier of Merchiston that Napier should help him to find a 'poise' of treasure supposed to be hidden in the castle or its grounds. Possibly Napier had in mind some form of divining – some early type of 'mine-detector', if you like – for the inventor of logarithms was an inventor in other ways too.

As the story goes, however, Logan soon poured scorn on Napier's methods, and Napier abandoned the project. All that is probably true. The written agreement is still in the Napier MSS and has been printed, with a facsimile, in Mark Napier's *Memoirs*. But, continues the story, as Napier left the castle (doubtless having drawn his 'expenses', as laid down in the agreement) he told Logan that if he wanted magic to help him to find his treasure, he should go to his kinswoman, Barbara Napier, and he'd get magic enough. Again probably true. Barbara Napier, as you know, was one of the famous coven of North Berwick witches who were accused in 1590 and 1591 of trying to raise a storm to wreck James VI's ship, or that of his bride, when the King and his Queen were on their way to Scotland from Denmark. And while most of the witches were put to death, Barbara Napier was lucky enough to be acquitted – though the jury themselves got into trouble for their clemency.

The next bit, I agree, is less well authenticated; but you will soon see how closely it fits in with a well-known fact.

Logan, it is said, did consult Barbara Napier, who gave him a large black dog which, she averred, would scent out the treasure for him. More than that, she assured him that the dog would henceforth be the guardian of Wolf's Crag, and would never cease to guard it until, so she said, 'your bones find their last resting-place in your grave.'

Now witches throughout all history have been credited with double meanings in their words and prophecies; and if there is any truth at all in this part of the legend or tradition, here was a double meaning with a vengeance. For Logan's bones never found 'their last resting-place in his grave'. In 1609 Logan, then dead, was accused for 'art and part' in the Gowrie Conspiracy; his bones were dug up from his grave and brought into court for trial in accordance with the Scottish law of treason; and, since he was found guilty, his bones were not returned to his grave.

So the black dog, whether or not it had scented out the treasure (and the local tradition is silent on that), and whether or not it had ceased to watch Wolf's Crag during the years that elapsed between Logan's death and the exhumation of his bones (and on that too the local tradition is silent), again became the guardian of the castle in 1609. Logan's bones, to stress Barbara Napier's *ipsissima verba*, had not found 'their last resting-place' in his grave.

Of the holding and haunting by the black dog, I need tell you little. Tradition has it that for long the whole neighbourhood was terrified. At night, the dog could be heard baying to the moon – a chilling sound even when it's an ordinary inoffensive dog that's doing the baying, but unnerving in the extreme when it's a hell-hound and the undying gift of a witch. By the day, no one dared to approach the place.

It is said that upon one occasion a cottar, living in the nearby steading at Dowlaw, who had been kept awake all one night by the dog's baying, vowed the next morning that he would 'finish' the dog and be done with it. Despite all attempts to hold him back, the cottar went down to the castle on his self-appointed task. He did not return; and no one had the courage to seek him in the precincts, or even the vicinity, of Wolf's Crag. Three days later, however, he was found far inland, wandering about the fields, half-naked, and a gibbering idiot unable to put two words together to make sense. More than that, although he lived on for several years, tended by his wife and children, the raw wound of a bite on his neck, perilously close to the trachea, would never heal, but continued to fester until the day of his death.

Even Cromwell's troops avoided the place in 1650, despite all their outward assurances of spiritual protection.

Then, to stay in those parts, came the Reverend David Home, fearless covenanter and field-preacher – a man whom no decree of the Privy Council could silence in his preaching and, *a fortiori*, a man who could allow no agent of the devil to be at work in his own 'parish'. Once again a man went down alone to face the black dog of Wolf's Crag: and this time it was the minister, armed only with his Bible and his bands.

When, after many hours, the minister returned, the whole of his people, men, women and children, were awaiting him; and, sore afraid, they had stood at a safe distance, their hours of waiting being spent in prayer and the singing of psalms. Slowly, and with great effort, the minister climbed the path towards them. They ran to meet him and, as they drew nearer, they could see that his face was drawn and white, while his eyes shone within it like great coals of fire. But, to all their questionings, he would only answer with the same words: 'The Lord hath prevailed. Blessed be the name of the Lord.'

It was a story well worthy of inclusion in Wodrow's 'Analecta';[6] it was no wonder his fellow preachers likened him to Benaiah, in the Book of Samuel, who, alone, went down and slew a lion in the midst of a pit in time of snow. Certainly, from that day onwards the black dog of Wolf's Crag troubled the people no more.

Later, in his field conventicles, the minister spoke at times in slightly greater detail, but always in the language of the Old Testament. A few of his sermons were printed in the collection called *The Head of the Corner*, and there you will notice two interesting references. In the one, he says: 'Even as Joshua commanded great stones to be rolled to the mouth of the cave that the five kings of Makkedah might be imprisoned therein, so did the Lord command me when I had overcome the beast of Baal'; in the other: 'The Lord did deliver him into my hands, and like unto the king of Ai the stones were raised over him.' Gradually it became known that when he had overcome the black dog of Wolf's Crag (and the secret of his victory died with him), the minister had cast it into an aumbry in one of the castle walls and had sealed up the opening with stones.

And that aumbry is still there, in the ruins, and still sealed up.

———

'And you say the aumbry is still there, and still walled-up?' asked someone.

Henderson nodded.

'And no one has had the curiosity, and the courage, to remove the stones to see if there is anything behind them?' put in Drummond.

'No,' replied Henderson. 'At least, not so far as I know. Despite the National Education Acts, the march of science, and so forth, the local people still believe the story of the dog and, if you like, still think it better to leave well alone. Even the Ministry of Works may have had somewhat similar thoughts. Certainly when the ruins of the castle were placed under the guardianship of the Ancient Monuments Board, and various repairs were carried out, the aumbry was left as it was.'

So the talk went on, this way and that. And, amid it all, I little thought that within a few days Davidson and I would be opening up that aumbry ourselves – only to wish we had left it alone, and now to wonder where our folly will end.

I had picked up Davidson in my car and we had driven out to Dunbar to look at the old town wall which was under a threat of demolition. We had seen what we wanted to see; we had spoken to a number of people who were in favour of preservation; we had had lunch; and it was still early afternoon. It was then that Davidson suggested a visit to Wolf's Crag, and I readily concurred. I simply wanted to see a walled-up aumbry and nothing more.

On the way there, I again heard the story of the black dog – exactly as Henderson had told it. I knew I would, for Davidson has forgotten more about the ruined abbeys and castles of Scotland than the rest of us have ever learned. But I wasn't prepared for what followed.

'I've often felt like removing those stones,' he concluded, 'just to see if there's anything behind them. I'm willing to wager that whatever may be there it won't be the skeleton of a dog.'

And with that I made our first mistake.

'I've got an old entrenching-tool in the boot of the car,' I said, rashly.

'Good!' he cried, with enthusiasm. 'We'll do it this very afternoon. I'll shoulder all the responsibility with the Ancient Monuments people. Though if we replaced the stones I doubt if anyone would be any the wiser.'

It was settled as easily and as unexpectedly as that. These things usually are. We regret our temerity afterwards.

So, on a sunny afternoon in June, the two of us stood before a walled-up aumbry in the ruins of Wolf's Crag. And I had an old entrenching-tool in my hand.

Everything seemed peaceful enough, with a calm water and

the sea-birds wheeling overhead. Though I'll admit I felt more keyed-up than I would have been had I been standing ready to remove any other walling in any other ruined castle. Almost certainly Davidson felt the same. It was natural it should be so. We both knew the story of that aumbry too well.

Then Davidson reached out his hand. He took the tool from me and inserted its smaller pick-like end in between two of the stones in the topmost course. That was simple enough, for it was 'dry-stone' walling, tightly packed with stones of smaller size; but although Davidson picked out the packing fairly easily and could bring a good pressure to bear on his chosen stone, somehow or other it seemed immovable. Muttering to himself, he chipped out more of the packing and tried again. Still the stone refused to move. I remember thinking that if the Reverend David Home had laid those stones he had laid and packed them well.

In the end we took it in turns. Both of us had the feeling we were not going to be defeated. Possibly it was that which deflected us from the wiser course. As it was, we levered and prised at that stone for perhaps half an hour, sweating and grunting as we worked, until at last it began to move.

Yet even when the stone appeared loose enough to be drawn out easily, it seemed to come unwillingly, almost as though someone or something were contesting it with us. Then, suddenly, it came out, so suddenly that it slipped through our hands and fell to the ground with a thud, leaving an opening in the wall, perhaps nine or ten inches square. And at once we both stepped back and looked at one another.

'What was that?' asked Davidson, sharply.

'I don't know,' I answered.

We were both shaken. Both of us had distinctly heard a rustling sound coming from the back of the barrier which we had breached with the removal of one stone.

'Maybe a bit of paper inside which moved with the change in the air,' said Davidson, though I could catch the lack of conviction in his voice. He knew as well as I did that the rustle of a piece of paper could not have reached our ears through that one hole in the topmost course.

Nor was that all.

Still looking tensely at the opening we had made, we saw something curling out, something like a wisp of black smoke, which rose in the air and, strangely, seemed to stay there, gathering itself together into a rough shape. And, with it, there came a stench I can never describe. It was not of this earth of ours and, because of that, man has never invented the words to define it. To say it was foul, like the stench of a vast mass of corruption, would still be an understatement.

On the instant both of us bent down for the fallen stone. Both of us had the one thought and the one thought only. That opening must be blocked up again – immediately, quickly, at once. Somewhat to our surprise, the stone went in easily; and we packed it as tightly as we could. It looked very much as it had looked before.

'Never again,' said Davidson, wiping his brow. 'Henceforth I shall keep to the motto: "Let sleeping dogs lie."'

'And so shall I,' came my immediate response. 'More than that, though I'd hate to be called a coward, I have a feeling I'd be glad to be back in the car.'

'So you feel that way, too?' he answered, looking me straight in the face. 'I don't know what it is. I've been here often enough before, but now I want to be away and out of it. And what's more, out of it quickly.'

Without another word he marched straight out of the ruins, while I followed closely at his heels. Once, I looked back. I could no longer see that strange shape of black smoke. It had gone.

We were perhaps half-way back to the car, with Davidson striding ahead, when, behind me, I heard the steady pat-pattering of a dog! Following us! Barbara Napier's dog! Losing all control of myself I ran for the car, calling out to Davidson as

I passed him on the path. Reaching the car, I pulled open the driver's door and tumbled in, shutting the door with a bang. Only then did I begin to recover.

Feeling safe again, and, perhaps because of that, feeling also somewhat ashamed, I looked back to the path. Davidson was still plodding steadily on. Hadn't he heard that dog pattering behind us? Had I simply imagined it all? Nerves, and nothing more? Or was it merely an ordinary dog that had run up for a moment towards us and had then turned off on its own intents and purposes?

'Running that last bit for exercise?' asked Davidson as he opened the door beside me but, I noticed, quickly shutting it behind him. 'I don't blame you. I felt like running myself. But I was damned if I would. And don't ask me why I felt like running. I don't know.'

'You didn't hear anything, then?' I queried, slowly.

'No,' he replied. 'Only the beating of my heart. I heard that well enough. But again don't ask me why. All I can tell you is that I didn't like the atmosphere down there one little bit. "Let sleeping dogs lie," did I say? Somehow I have a feeling that I wish we had.'

'We'll go,' I said tersely, starting the car. I did not tell him of the pat-pattering that had put me to shameful flight.

We removed that stone a week ago. And today, by post, I received from Davidson a copy of the *East Lothian and Berwickshire Advertiser* in which he had marked two passages. I can now recite them by heart:

LOCAL NEWS
Wolf's Crag

Yesterday two visitors to Wolf's Crag were savagely attacked by a large black dog which appeared to have assumed the duty of guarding the entrance to the ruins. Fortunately both of them had walking-sticks and they were able to some extent to protect themselves. As it was, however, one of them had to be treated by a doctor for a severe bite in the shoulder, and both of them are suffering from shock. (*See Editorial Comment, p.3.*)

EDITORIAL
Wolf's Crag

Under our Local News we print an account of an attack by a large black dog on two visitors to the ruined castle of Wolf's Crag. Our readers may be interested to know that according to local tradition Wolf's Crag was at one time long defended by another 'black dog' which was the terror of the countryside and which was reputed to have been given by a witch to Logan of Restalrig, the then holder of the castle. Fortunately we live in the twentieth century and have no longer to contend with witches and their spells. We understand that the Ministry of Works and the S.S.P.C.A. have been informed of this attack, and it should not be long before the dog now at the ruins is either trapped or killed.

————••••••————

In this second paragraph the words 'another black dog' were heavily underlined and following the final sentence were the words, in Davidson's handwriting: 'I hope to God he is right!'

Let the Dead Bury the Dead

Let the Dead Bury the Dead

'HAS AN ARCHAEOLOGIST any qualms when he is excavating an early burial?' asked MacEwen, turning to our Professor of Prehistory. 'Do the bones ever give you the creeps?'

Abercrombie paused before answering. A long pause.

'Sometimes,' he conceded at last. 'I had a grim experience when I was still a young lecturer. And, to be frank, that's why I concentrated on iron-age forts and, for some twenty years, left burials severely alone.'

'Tell us more,' put in Drummond, settling himself in his chair. 'And don't spare the gruesome details.'

'Not gruesome, but tragic,' Abercrombie replied. 'And since the whole affair took place some thirty years ago I see no reason why I shouldn't tell you about it.'

⁕

As I said, I was a young lecturer at the time, a mere beginner, when, one day, to my utter surprise, I received a letter from Hawthorn inviting me to help him with the excavation of a small group of early bronze age burials on which he was already at work. Naturally I accepted at once. Hawthorn's name will be known to you. He was a brilliant archaeologist, with a European reputation. Here was my chance. But I wish I could have had some foreknowledge of what was to come.

I was met at a lonely wayside station. Hawthorn loaded my things on to an old army truck, and we drove off. But, after his first greeting, I found him strangely silent. My efforts at conversation drooped and dragged. I felt myself chattering, and gave up. 'He's looking much older,' I thought. 'Probably doing too much.'

Hawthorn turned the truck off the main road and followed a rough track across the moor. Mile after mile: and each mile taking us further into complete isolation in a bleak and desolate land. A white speck appeared in the distance. It was Hawthorn's tent. He stopped the truck beside it and we clambered out. All around us lay one vast expanse of heather, bog and tussocky grass, studded here and there with the rough shapes of massive boulders which, in the half-light of the evening, became strangely menacing and looked like huge monsters, crouching, ready to spring. A few black-faced sheep moving and nibbling amongst them were oddly reassuring. I shook myself as though wishing to be rid of an uneasy burden.

'I had no idea you were as isolated as this,' I said, glad even of the sound of my own voice. 'You must have felt pretty lonely.'

'Yes,' he answered slowly, and then, suddenly: 'That's why I asked you to come. Though I need your help too,' he continued quickly. 'There are possibly ten or a dozen burials. They all seem to be near the surface, but two workers are better than one.'

'But did you come here all by yourself?' I persisted. 'Surely you had someone with you at the start.'

I had an idea that he glanced at me sideways, and then looked away. There was a perceptible pause.

'Chalmers was with me for a while. In fact he came with me. But he had to go away. So I wrote to you.'

This time I was sure he gave me a quick, almost guilty look, before deliberately turning away and walking to the opening of the tent.

'I am glad you did,' I answered, following him. 'I've seen two or three isolated graves, but I've never seen a collective group of them. Is there a stone circle of any kind round them? Anything in the nature of a temenos? They certainly chose a desolate place for their burials,' I continued, looking at the wild expanse all around.

Again there was a pause until, turning from the tent, he said: 'Yes, it *is* desolate. And the only living soul I've met is a shepherd who comes to see me every day. Every day, I tell you, almost as though wanting to be sure I'm still alive. And I am still alive,' he added, fiercely.

I looked at him in astonishment.

'I'm sorry,' he said, his voice normal again. 'Nerves. Never suffered from them before. But this place is becoming too much for me. Bring your traps into the tent. When we've had something to eat, I'll make my confession. Did you bring the tinned stuff I suggested?'

'It's all here,' I answered. 'Can I help you with the meal? Where do you get your water?'

'Over there,' he said, pointing the way. 'You'll find a small burn and a pool into which you can dip the can easily. I'll get it for you.'

He disappeared into the tent and came back with the can.

'Don't be too long,' he cautioned, and then smiled wanly. 'I'm not afraid of being left alone. Not yet, at any rate. But it's nearly dark already, and if you're too long you may find yourself floundering in and out of peat-bogs on your way back.'

I took the can, filled it at the burn (which I found without difficulty) and made my way back. He was awaiting me, standing in front of the tent and holding a lantern which he had lit. It was hardly yet dark enough for me to need the guidance of the light, but I appreciated his thought.

'We'll need it for our meal,' he said, almost apologetically. 'You found the burn all right?' I held up the can as witness to my success. He nodded approvingly. 'Come then, we'll get our meal ready.'

Shown where to find this, and where to find that, I half-hindered, half-helped in the preparations. In due course, however, we were sitting at the table of an upturned box and consuming an excellent supper. The meal over, we filled the dirty pots and pans with the remainder of the water and placed them outside, to be washed in the burn on the morrow. We closed the flap of the tent, sat on our respective camp-beds, and literally looked at one another.

'Do you mind if we have a drink?' he asked, breaking the silence. 'It's not become a habit, I assure you. But I think it would help me to tell you the more easily why I asked you to come.'

He produced a bottle of whisky and poured out two quite ordinary tots. I was relieved to notice their moderation.

'Confusion to our enemies,' I said, holding up my glass.

'And knowledge as to who they are,' came his odd response. 'And now I'll confess,' he continued, putting down his glass and sitting to face me squarely across the upturned box.

'I came here just over a fortnight ago, intending, as you know from my letter, to excavate this group of early bronze age burials. They are referred to in an old local history, published about 1820 – it was Ross of Aberdeen who gave me the reference – but nobody seems to have thought of excavating them until quite recently. In fact, when I came here, I thought I was going to be the first to open them. But I was wrong.'

He paused there, took another sip at his whisky and paused again, as though wondering how to continue.

'It was the shepherd who told me of the other man,' he continued. 'Apparently last year another archaeologist was here, and opened two of the graves. As soon as I examined the site I could see that two excavations had been made and then closed in again. But when, as my first task, I reopened those two graves, I didn't like them one little bit. Yet in the end I succeeded in persuading myself that this is the middle of the twentieth century; that such "things" don't happen; and that I wasn't going to be put off anyway.

'You see when I reopened the first of those two graves it looked exactly as though the burial had been made last year instead of, say, three thousand five hundred years ago. The bones lay there in perfect position – the usual doubled-up posture of a "short cist" with the knees drawn up to the chin – but they lay there in a new grave. The stones lining the grave and covering it in were not only in perfect position, but they were new and newly-laid. It was a new grave for old bones. There was no possibility of my being mistaken. In some way at which I cannot even guess, those old bones, dried, shrunk and friable as they were, had been carefully and reverently reburied in a newly-made cist.

'But who had done it? And why? And how? It was certainly not done by my predecessor on the site. I tell you, he couldn't have done it. It was then that I had my first wild thoughts which I strove to thrust aside. But can you imagine my thoughts when I reopened my predecessor's second excavation and found that that, too, was a reburial in a newly-made grave? You may think you can, but you haven't heard yet what the shepherd said.'

His voice was rising again. I put out a reassuring hand and said: 'Some old wives' tale, I'll be bound. But why let it worry you?'

'Yes,' he replied more calmly. 'I must keep a grip on myself if I'm to see this through. And I'm determined to see it through – if

I can.' He poured out another small tot of whisky and sipped it slowly, forcing himself into composure.

'You see the shepherd insists that the place is holy. Has some sort of voodoo on it, if I may use that word in its vulgar sense. That no one can desecrate a grave with impunity, however old the grave may be. That the dead still protect the dead. And so forth and so on. He started the very first day I came. Scared Chalmers somewhat, though Chalmers didn't leave me then. I'll come to that later. He repeated it, with additions, when I'd reopened the first of those two graves. He repeated it, with more additions, when I'd reopened the second one, and I was more than a bit scared myself. Then he told me of the other man. How he'd done his best to persuade him to leave the graves alone and to go away. Just as he was trying to persuade me to pack up and go away. But the other fellow refused to listen. Just as I was refusing to listen. So the dead took matters into their own dead hands . . .'

'Steady,' I murmured.

'It appears that the day after the other fellow had opened the second grave the shepherd couldn't find him on his daily visit. For that persistent shepherd, mark you, had looked him up every day – just as he looks me up! And the day after the opening of the second grave the shepherd couldn't find him anywhere. He was not in his tent; he was not at the site. But he was found all right. Lying by a clump of heather within a stone's throw of the graves he'd desecrated. Just lying there, dead.'

I gave a start.

'Yes,' he said, 'it must have been Fairbairn. I haven't checked up the dates, but they are close enough. And you have remembered as quickly as I did that last year Fairbairn was found dead on some excavation which he was conducting alone and that there was a somewhat unsatisfactory inquiry into the cause of his death. But I didn't know it was here, on this very site.'

'And you still want to go on?' I asked slowly.

'Yes,' he almost shouted. 'The whole damned thing must be sheer nonsense. I refuse to let a shepherd's silly talk put me off. In fact I've already opened a third grave,' he continued, more quietly. 'Finished the excavation this morning before you arrived. As good a short cist as you'd ever hope to see, and nothing queer about it either. The stones lining it look as old as the hills, and the skeleton is all tumbled in upon itself. I tell you I shall go on until I've excavated the whole lot or until something else happens – to me.'

He paused there, and then went on. 'But I must have some help. That's why I invited you to join me. Though I can tell you I didn't write to you without asking myself again and again whether it was fair of me to bring you here at all.'

'But how did you come to pick on me?' I asked, seeking to solve my own petty problem.

'Well,' he answered slowly, 'in the first place I guessed you'd got good nerves. Had to have in the sort of job you did in the war. And in the second place, you've got a medical degree and,' he continued, looking me straight in the eye, 'if anything should happen to me, well, I'd have a fully qualified doctor on the spot – even if all he could do would be to sign my death certificate.'

'Nonsense!' I replied quickly, though somehow or other that one word didn't sound anything like so convincing as it should have done. 'But why did Chalmers leave?'

'Oh, Chalmers. Poor beggar. He was looking over his shoulder before we'd finished reopening the first of Fairbairn's two graves. That shepherd's talk got on his nerves far more than it got on mine. He left when we had just started on Fairbairn's second excavation – all because a stone fell on his foot. Said it couldn't have fallen. It was against the law of gravity. Said it must have been pushed. And as I hadn't pushed it, who had? For all he knew, the next one would be pushed to fall on his head and crack his skull. I think I lost my temper. At any rate, off he went. Forthwith. Rather childishly, I refused to drive him to the station. So he took just what he could carry and most needed, and marched away.

'But I shall still go on. I've made up my mind. Possibly I shouldn't have asked you to come. Perhaps I should have told you all this in my letter. But how could I? And what would you have thought of it, if I had? I've roughly filled in those first two graves. Better hide that evidence – whatever it may mean. But, as I told you, I've opened a third grave, and there's nothing queer about that. You can see it for yourself tomorrow. The stones in that one are not newly-laid. No new cist for old bones there. Old stones and old bones – fallen, and scattered. You'll stay to see that one, won't you? Though if, after all you know now, you want to go back home first thing tomorrow morning I'd be the last to blame you. And,' he added, with a ghost of a smile, 'I'll drive you back to the station with all your things.'

There was only one answer to that. I gave it. But I could not help thinking that had his letter told me even a little of all this, I might not have posted my acceptance as quickly as I had done only two days earlier.

'Good,' he said. 'We'll look at my third grave and the whole of the site tomorrow morning. But let's change the topic. This queer business so dogs my mind that I could go on talking about it all night and for ever. And can you wonder? But now you're here we can at least have some rational conversation even if other things seem to be wholly irrational. How is your work getting on? You were doing something on those ring-forts in Perthshire, weren't you?'

For a while we talked of this and that; of my own work; of archæological studies in general. A little scandal; a little gossip. It was after midnight when we both turned in and Hawthorn blew out the lantern.

But although our concluding talk had been of other things, that earlier talk still dominated my mind. I lay awake trying to make sense of it all. Had Hawthorn – and Chalmers – just imagined things? Had Hawthorn been overworking? And was this the result? He was certainly in an excitable state and 'living on his nerves'. A companion would do him good. A gentle sedative mightn't be a bad thing either. But was it all imagination? Would I stay if anything else happened? And yet why should it?

--- ·•᎒᎒᎒•· ---

How long I lay awake with these and similar thoughts I do not know. All I know is that I fell asleep at last, that I had no bad dreams, and that next morning I awoke in the strange light always caused by the sun shining through tent-canvas.

I looked at my wrist-watch. It said almost eleven o'clock. I sat up at once and looked across the tent to Hawthorn's bed. It was empty. Good fellow! He had left me to do the sleeping while he did the chores.

I dressed slowly and strolled out of the tent. It was a lovely day – blazing sun, clear sky, and a refreshing, slight north-east wind. Then my eye caught something on the ground just by the tent. Our dirty pots and pans. Well, at least I could wash those out in the burn. But where was Hawthorn? Probably gone to look at his graves, I thought. Should I try to find him? Or should I just wash the dishes and wait for him to come back? We'd need them for breakfast anyway.

Breakfast! With a start, I suddenly realized we ought to have had breakfast long ago. Hawthorn ought to have awakened me. Where was Hawthorn? A sentence from our talk flashed through my mind. 'The dead still protect the dead.' And at once, pursuing it, came a second searing sentence: 'Let the dead bury the dead.' Even as they had reburied the dead of those two desecrated graves!

I was nearly in a panic then. But not quite. Calling myself a fool and pulling myself together, I decided I'd be certain to find Hawthorn at his excavation and probably completely oblivious of the time. Well, I'd find him first, and then we'd have breakfast together. But where was his excavation? He'd never told me last night. I'd need to look for it.

I found his excavation, and I found him there. He was lying huddled-up beside a newly-opened grave, and I knew at once that he was dead. I went down on my knees beside him, but I could find no cause of death. He was unmarked: and his face was serene.

Then, as I bent to lift him up, my glance fell upon that newly-opened grave. Hawthorn's third. The one he was to show me this very day. Startled, I looked again; for that grave was far different from the description he had given me only a few hours before. *The bones lying there were in perfect position, and the stones lining the grave were clean, new, and newly-laid.*

The Castle Guide

The Castle Guide

MANY YEARS AGO, in the deepening dusk of a June evening, I was strolling past the Castle of St Andrews when I noticed that, strangely, the admission-gate was still open. Attracted by the grey and sombre ruins, silhouetted against the darkening sky, I stopped at the open gate. If I were to venture inside, what strange shadows would I see? How different would those broken walls and towers appear?

Sauntering down to the pend, I passed through its deep-black vault and out into the castle-close. There, spell-bound by a beauty and mystery that were enhanced by the fading light, I stood for a while motionless. Below me I could hear the rhythmic plash of the sea on the rocks that bore the castle's weight, while the light sough of the wind could have come from the ancient stones themselves, whispering to one another their memories of the past. And soon, caught in the magic of the place, I began to give words and meaning to the sounds that came and went:

'Beaton, proud Roman Cardinal, murdered and defiled.'

'Guns, French guns, breaking down block-house and tower.'

'Knox, John Knox, toiling at the galley's oar.'

So I let my fancies free until, upon an instant, every fancy fled. A man, in the dress of a mid-sixteenth century man-at-arms, was standing in front of me.

Startled, I stepped back; for the man had appeared as suddenly as if the shadows themselves had formed and fashioned him. And why was he dressed like that? Then came sudden relief. I remembered that a pageant was to be held on the castle-green. I had intruded at the close of a dress-rehearsal, and here was the last of the actors about to leave. And that, too, explained the open admission-gate.

Recovering myself, I said: 'Good evening.' The man answered with a nod and then, in the broadest Scots I had ever heard, offered to show me the eastern block-house that had fallen beneath the battery of the French guns. Somewhat puzzled – for I knew that nothing was left of the eastern block-house, and that even its site was conjectural – and not sure that I had understood his invitation aright, I stammered politely: 'Why, yes; certainly'; and then could have kicked myself. The man would probably be both an ignoramus and a bore. However, I would get away from him as quickly as I could. I glanced furtively at my watch. The time was five minutes to ten. I would give him until five minutes past ten, and would then make some excuse to escape.

But I had to make no excuse.

My self-appointed guide led me across the castle-green and up to the ruined eastern range. There, as soon as we had reached the wall, he began to describe in vivid detail the French bombardment which, in July 1547, had brought a year-long siege to an end. At times his broad Scots was beyond me, but somehow that seemed to make no difference. So graphic was his account, as he stood beside me, with his arm outstretched and his finger pointing into space, that a block-house rose up and took shape before my eyes. I sensed, rather than heard, the noise of the guns; and I saw the building slowly crumbling beneath their battery. I could even see men falling and dying as their strongpoint collapsed around them.

Suddenly his story came to an abrupt end. He turned and left me, and, as I watched him walking slowly across the castle-close, the shadows seemed to fold around him. He entered the dark places, he was lost in them, and he never reappeared.

For a moment, I felt as though I had awakened from some strange and uncanny dream. I looked again over the eastern wall. No longer did I see a block-house crumbling beneath the battery of cannons royal. Before me was only the empty space of night, while, in the near distance, I glimpsed the tall broken gables of the cathedral church.

A vague sense of wonder gave way to fear. How could it have been a dream when I had been wide-awake all the time? What had happened to me? Who had stood beside me and shown me a building that was no longer there? My fear increased. An impelling urge to escape took hold of me. I must get out! But how could I pass through that forbidding blackness of the pend? What hand would reach out to hold me back?

Bracing myself, I ran; ran as fast as I could, speeding through the pend, up the slope of the path, and out into the safety of the street. There, for a minute or two, I clutched the railings with both hands. I had no body; only my two hands that were clutching the iron railings and a heart that pounded violently.

Yet, quickly, I recovered. I began to damn myself. I was an idiot, a coward, a craven fool. Leaving the friendly railings, I walked slowly down the street, though my mind still raced with disturbing thoughts. As I neared Butts Wynd, the clocks began to strike. I looked at my watch. It said ten o'clock. Incredulous, I counted the strokes that rang through the night. Ten o'clock. Had time stood still while a ghostly guide had taken me four centuries back in time? I had looked at my watch when he first spoke to me only five minutes ago. Yet he had spoken to me for perhaps ten minutes, or a quarter of an hour. And definitely a full five minutes had elapsed since I ran in panic from the castle-close.

Perplexed and disturbed, I turned into the narrow wynd. So, trying vainly to find reason in something that was beyond all reasoning, I began to wander through the streets of the town –

down North Street, up Market Street, down South Street, and on to the West Port. There, just as I had passed through the narrow archway of the Port, someone suddenly gripped me by the arm. I looked up, with a start. It was my old friend, James Davidson, who was then still in office as H.M. Chief Inspector of Ancient Monuments.

'Whither away with fast shut eyes?' he cried.

I do not remember what answer I gave; but he looked more sharply at me, and drew me closer to him.

'What's wrong with you, man?' he asked. 'You look as though you've seen a ghost.'

'I have,' I replied, 'in the castle-close.'

'A likely enough place,' he said, gravely.

'But, Jamie, this one spoke to me. Told me how the east block-house had been battered to bits by the French guns, and pointed it out to me as the guns were smashing it down. I tell you I saw that block-house with my own eyes, saw it gradually crumbling away, and saw the men falling and dying. And all the while time stood still.'

'Steady, old man. Time doesn't stand still. When did this happen? Just now?'

'Yes,' I answered. 'At five minutes to ten.'

I felt his hold tighten on my arm.

'You say you met your ghost at five minutes to ten?'

'Yes,' I persisted. 'I looked at my watch.'

'Good God!' I heard him mutter.

'Why? What?' I demanded, quickly.

'The old custodian of the castle once told me exactly what the eastern block-house looked like, and where it had stood,' he said, quietly.

'But what has that to do with it?'

He paid no attention to my question, but went on, as though talking to himself: 'And when I asked him how he could possibly know, he just looked at me in a queer sort of way and said: "I can't tell you, sir. But sometimes, if I stand on the eastern range when night is falling, I have a feeling I've been there before – long, long ago.'"

I grew impatient.

'But this wasn't your custodian, Jamie. It was a ghost, I tell you. A ghost that came out of the shadows and returned to the shadows again. The ghost of a man-at-arms who'd taken part in the siege of 1547.'

'I know,' he replied. 'But it was my custodian all the same. I've just come from the old man's house. He died at five minutes to ten.'

The Witch's Bone

The Witch's Bone

MICHAEL ELLIOTT, M.A., LL.D., F.S.A. (SCOT.), frowned at the letter which had come from the Honorary Curator of the local Museum. It was quite a short letter and quite a simple one: merely asking him if he would allow the Museum to borrow his 'Witch's Bone' for a special exhibition covering Folk Beliefs and Customs. But Michael Elliott found the letter far from welcome. Short and simple as it was, it revived and increased all the fearful troubles of his mind. More than that, dare he now let the 'Bone' pass out of his own keeping – even if only for a little while?

Every day, for the last week, that witch's bone had preoccupied his mind to the exclusion of all else. The witch's bone that had brought to an end all his quarrels with Mackenzie Grant. The witch's bone that had possibly given him a revenge far more terrible than anything he had sought or expected. In a fit of anger he had thought only of testing its efficacy, never really believing it would work. And now he knew that the bone had worked only too well. Or had it? Had he indeed compassed Grant's death? All he knew was that Grant had died and that now he found it hard to recover his peace of mind.

Of course, he had only himself to blame. He had shown the bone at the last meeting of their local Antiquarian Society, just after he had acquired it; and, pleased with himself, he had expatiated upon its awful power. Mackenzie Grant had contradicted him – as usual. Grant had always treated his theories with contempt. There was his paper on lake-dwellings, and, after that, his paper on the iron-age forts in the Central Highlands. Upon both occasions Grant had stood up and pooh-poohed everything he had said. At meetings of the Council, too, the man could be relied upon to speak against anything he proposed. But all that was past history. Grant had poured scorn upon his story of the bone. And now Grant was dead. Yet how unbounded would be the relief to his tortured mind if Grant had been right, and if the story of the bone were 'stuff and nonsense' and nothing more. The very night that Grant had ridiculed his story he had put the bone to the test, directing its malevolent powers against Mackenzie Grant. And Grant had died a horrible death a few hours later. But could it not have been a ghastly coincidence in which the bone had played no part at all?

It was only a short piece of bone – probably sheep-bone – about six inches long, with a narrow ring of black bog-oak tightly encircling it near its centre. He had acquired it during his recent holiday in Sutherland. An old woman had died in a remote glen, and, because she had been reputed to be a witch, and had been feared as such, no one would bear her to burial. The local minister had called upon him, beseeching his help. 'The poor body was no witch at all,' the minister had said. 'She was just old and ill-favoured. I have had a coffin made of about the right size – at any rate it will be large enough – and if you could just drive me to the old body's hut, with the coffin in the rear of your estate-wagon, maybe we could manage to coffin her and give her a Christian burial.'

A strange request to make of any man! But the minister had won him over, and his reward had been the witch's bone.

They had found it on a shelf in the old woman's hut. The minister had seen it first, and had prodded it gently with his finger. 'So,' he had said softly. 'The witch's bone. I have been told of it. There are those of my people who say that she would utter her curse upon some man or woman, and then would make a wax figure and stick a pin into it. Then they say that if this bone rattled on its shelf, she knew that her curse had taken effect and that the person portrayed in the wax would be seized with pains in that part of the body which corresponded with the place of the pin in the wax. Some have even said that she could kill by sticking her pin in the heart or the head. For the power is in the bone. It can wound or kill any who are cursed by its possessor. And never are they spared.'

He had listened and looked with astonishment until, suddenly, the minister's face had changed and he had cried out: 'But what am I saying to you? There is no Witch of Endor in Sutherland. Indeed there is not. No such devilry is possible. I am not believing one word of it.' And the minister had boldly picked up the bone and had offered it to him. 'Take it with you,' he had said. 'It may interest some of your friends in the south.' And, wondering, he had taken it.

Yes; it had interested some of his friends. But Mackenzie Grant had laughed at him. 'A witch's bone!' he had said, contemptuously. 'Stuff and nonsense. Anyone can see by just looking at it that it's a handle, and nothing more. That ring round its centre simply means that, when it is grasped, two fingers go on one side of the ring, and two fingers on the other. Any boy, flying a kite, grasps a piece of wood in exactly the same way at the end of his string. A witch's bone, indeed. I believe, Elliott, I could persuade you that a handkerchief with a hole in it is a witch's veil to be worn at meetings of her coven. And the hole, of course, would be symbolic, indicative of her lapse from the Christian faith.' And so the man had gone on. Laughing at him before his friends.

He had kept down the anger which had surged within him; but, when he had returned home, and had taken the bone from his pocket, all his pent-up feelings had broken their bounds. He had marched straight into his study and, placing the bone upon a bookshelf near the fireplace, had resolved to prove its power to hurt. Aloud and deliberately he had cursed Mackenzie Grant; but, searching for sealing-wax, could find none. Then he had recalled the photograph of Mackenzie Grant in a recent volume of the Transactions of their Society. He had recalled, too, his aversion to destroying any photograph. To tear up a photograph had always seemed to him to be akin to tearing the living flesh and bones, So much the better. Mackenzie Grant should be torn asunder with a vengeance.

He had ripped the full-page photograph from the book and had deliberately torn it to pieces. In the fury of his task he had, for the moment, forgotten the bone. But, as the torn pieces had multiplied between his hands, suddenly there had come a rattling sound from the nearby shelf. And, at that, his heart had turned to ice. Fearfully he had looked at the bone; but it lay exactly where he had placed it, and it lay inert and still. He remembered assuring himself that he had simply imagined that rattle. He was overwrought. Yes, it was imagination and nothing more.

Yet, the next morning, when reading the *Scotsman* at breakfast-time, again a chill had struck his heart and his whole body had numbed with fear. For the paper announced with regret that a distinguished antiquary, Mr Mackenzie Grant, had been killed in a road accident. According to the announcement, Mr Grant, when driving home about midnight, after having dined with a friend, had unaccountably run head-on into a heavy lorry that had stopped for some minor adjustment on the opposite side of the road. It was a bad accident. Grant's car had been completely telescoped. But, in the opinion of the doctors, he must have been killed instantaneously, for their examination showed that he had suffered multiple injuries and that practically every bone in his body was broken.

No wonder his mind was ill at ease. He had striven to

persuade himself that it was pure coincidence. That those multiple injuries had naught to do with a photograph torn into many shreds. He had laboured to free himself from a haunting burden of guilt. Yet the torturing thought was still there. Had the bone indeed the power of killing those who were cursed by its possessor?

Since then he had locked it up in his coin-cabinet. He had even been afraid to open the cabinet to make certain it was still there. And now the Museum had asked to be allowed to borrow it, to put it on display. To say he had lost it, or had destroyed it, would be childish. Yet dare he lend it? Dare he allow it to pass out of his own keeping?

These were but some of the thoughts that troubled the mind of Dr Michael Elliott as he sat with a letter that lay before him on his desk.

———— ••ৡৡ•• ————

About nine o'clock in the evening of the same day, when Sir Stephen Rowandson, C.I.E., the Honorary Curator of the Museum, was deep in a detective story, his housekeeper knocked on his study door and announced: 'Dr Michael Elliott.'

Somewhat surprised, Rowandson put down his book and rose to greet his visitor.

'Come in, Elliott. Come in. This is an unexpected pleasure.'

Michael Elliot entered the room slowly and hesitantly.

'Man, but you do look tired,' continued Rowandson, as Elliott came into the light. 'It's these cold nights. Take that chair by the fire and warm yourself. 'I'll get you a whisky.'

Elliott took the proffered chair and sank down in it. If, indeed, he was looking tired, he knew full well that it was not due to the coldness of the night.

'I've called about your letter, asking for the loan of my witch's bone,' he said, turning to his host and gratefully accepting the whisky which had been poured out for him. 'I thought I'd sooner bring it to you personally at your home, rather than give it to you, or leave it for you, at the Museum.'

'Why, certainly,' replied Rowandson, concealing his surprise. 'You think I might possibly leave it lying about in the Museum, and it might fall into the wrong hands?'

Rowandson spoke with a smile. But Elliott coloured slightly.

'You have guessed correctly. It may be more dangerous than we know.'

Rowandson looked more closely at his visitor. Did Elliott really believe that this bit of bone could exert occult force? He had been one of those standing by when Mackenzie Grant had poured scorn upon it; and although he had not heard Elliott's account of its supposed malignant power, he knew full well that the man was apt to be too credulous. But perhaps he had better humour him.

'You are right,' he conceded, gravely. 'I have seen some strange things myself in India. We must be careful. Would it make you happier if I promised that when I do put it on display I will put it in a locked case?'

Elliott's relief was too apparent to be disguised.

'I was hoping for something like that,' he said, taking the bone from his breast pocket. 'It is good of you to go to so much trouble; but I should feel reassured if it was under lock and key.'

'You can rely on me,' returned Rowandson. 'I will keep it safely here, in the house, until I have a locked case ready for it. And I will tell no one it is here.'

Once more Elliott's relief was so obvious that Rowandson, taking the bone from him, ostentatiously looked around his study for a safe keeping-place. Not finding one, he placed the bone on his desk. 'I'll find a safe place for it later,' he assured Elliott. 'You can rely on me. And I will certainly keep it here until I take it personally to the Museum and myself place it in a display case that can be securely locked.'

Thereafter, for some ten minutes or so, Sir Stephen Rowandson strove in vain to find some topic of conversation which would interest his visitor. But Elliott answered only in monosyllables, while his eyes constantly strayed to the witch's bone lying on the Curator's desk, and his only thought was whether he should warn Rowandson of its dangerous power, or whether that would merely make him look foolish and at the same time make Rowandson less responsive and also more careless.

'Well,' said Rowandson, as he wearied of his task. 'I mustn't keep you too late. And don't worry about your bone. It will be quite safe.'

Elliott rose heavily to his feet. 'Thank you,' he said. 'I am sorry to be so fussy, but, you know, I do believe it may be a witch's bone and not, as . . . as . . . Mackenzie Grant maintained, simply a handle of some kind.'

The last words had come out with difficulty, and Rowandson thought he understood.

'Yes, poor fellow. We shall miss his sceptical comments. We were all his victims at one time or another.'

Elliott winced. Again his eyes strayed to the witch's bone.

'You won't leave it there, will you?' he asked.

'No, no,' replied Rowandson, quickly. 'I'll find a safe place for it all right.'

Seemingly reassured, Elliott moved towards the door of the room. Rowandson opened it and, conducting his visitor through the hall, let him out of the house. For a minute or two he watched the retreating figure. 'There goes one of the most distinguished classical scholars in Europe,' he said to himself, 'and yet with more antiquarian bees in his bonnet than any man I know. A witch's bone, indeed. It may be. But, even so, what harm can it do to anyone?'

He returned to his study and, picking up the bone from his desk, examined it under the reading-lamp. But his examination made him no wiser.

'Well, well. Old Elliott was certainly mighty concerned about it, and I'd better do what I said. But where shall I put the wretched thing? I haven't a safe, and there isn't a drawer in the whole house that would defeat a ten-year-old.'

Moving about the room with the bone in his hand, Rowandson finally stopped in front of an old-fashioned knick-knack stand which bore on its shelves a medley of flints, cylindrical seals, Roman nails, and other small archaeological objects of varying periods and kinds. 'The very place,' he muttered. 'Not so much Poe's idea in *The Purloined Letter* as Chesterton's idea of hiding a leaf in a forest.'

By moving some of the specimens closer to one another he cleared a small space on one of the shelves and placed the bone there. Stepping back, he surveyed the result and found it good.

Two days later, as Sir Stephen Rowandson entered his study after a frugal breakfast, he was feeling thoroughly disgruntled. His housekeeper, summoned yesterday afternoon to nurse a sister who had suddenly been taken ill, had left him to fend for himself; and Sir Stephen Rowandson was not accustomed to domestic work. He had managed to prepare his coffee, toast and marmalade for breakfast; but now the dead ashes in his study fire-place mocked him. He would have to rake out those ashes and lay the fire himself. Unwillingly he began his task. As he busied himself with paper and firewood, his mind turned to the Museum and to his forthcoming exhibition. And his thoughts made him more disgruntled still. Why should everything go wrong at one and the same time? For, yesterday morning, when one or two members of the Society had come to the Museum to help with the final preparations, and when, in accordance with his promise, he had arranged for a place in one of the two locked cases to be reserved for Michael Elliott's witch's bone, the interfering and officious Colonel Hogan had actually presumed to give contrary orders, even asserting that the bone wasn't worth a place in the exhibition anywhere. He had had trouble with the Colonel before. The man seemed to think he was in command of everything. But this time there had followed an unseemly wrangle in which he had completely lost his temper. More than that, in defending his promise to Elliott, he had hotly argued that the bone might be more dangerous than any of them realized. That heated altercation had made him look foolish; and he remembered, to his annoyance, the glances that had been exchanged. The word would now go round that he was becoming as credulous as Elliott himself. But if Elliott hadn't been so fussy, the argument would never have started at all.

'I could curse the old fool,' he muttered angrily, as he thrust the sticks of firewood among the paper which he had crushed up and laid in the hearth. 'Damn Michael Elliott, and damn his bone.'

He finished laying the fire and rose up from his task when, as he did so, he heard a strange rattle which seemed to come from somewhere within the room. Startled, he looked round. But nothing had fallen; nothing seemed to be out of place. 'Probably a bird fluttered against the window,' he said, dubiously. 'But it didn't sound like it. It was a queer sound. Never heard anything like it before.'

Well, what now? He could go to the Museum and work there; then he could lunch at his Club; back to the Museum again; dinner at the Club; and perhaps he could even collect together a bridge-four for the evening. Yes, he could manage without his housekeeper for a day or two. But he hoped it wouldn't be longer than that.

———————··⚬⚬··———————

Everything had worked according to plan, and Sir Stephen Rowandson was feeling much happier. He had put in a good morning's work; he had had an excellent lunch at his Club – and had even arranged a bridge-four; he had carried on with his exhibition in the afternoon; and, to his great relief, the members who had dropped in to help had given no indication that yesterday's wrangle had affected them in any way at all. It was nearly five o'clock, and he was thinking of giving up for the day, when he heard the bell ring. That was unusual. Who could be ringing the bell? The door was open, and people just walked in. Somewhat puzzled, he went to the door and found there a young man.

'Sir Stephen Rowandson?'

'Yes.'

'My name is Robert Reid, sir. You won't know me, but I'm the local representative of the *Scotsman* and I was told you might be able to help me.'

Sir Stephen Rowandson led his visitor into the main room of the Museum.

'And what can I do to help you?' he asked.

'I'm anxious to trace a photograph of Dr Michael Elliott. The paper wishes to carry one tomorrow. I do not like to call at his house, and it was suggested to me that probably you would have one here since, or so I gather, Dr Elliott was a prominent member of your Society.'

'But why can't you call at his house?'

The young man looked up quickly.

'But of course, how stupid of me. You cannot have heard.' Then, in a slightly lower voice, he continued: 'I'm very sorry to tell you, sir, that Dr Michael Elliott is dead. He was killed in a bad accident in Edinburgh, about half-past eleven this morning. And, as you will understand, we must carry a fairly long obituary notice. We would also like a photograph, if possible.'

'Michael Elliott dead,' repeated Rowandson, dully.

'Yes, sir. Apparently he was walking along the pavement by a site where a new building is going up when, for some unknown reason, a steel girder that was being lifted by a crane slipped from the chains which were holding it. Hitting the side of the building, it slewed round and, by sheer bad luck, fell on Dr Elliott and crushed him to death.'

'How horrible!'

'Yes, sir. But we are told that death must have been instantaneous. For not only was Dr Elliott badly crushed but also the girder, in falling, broke down a wooden screen which was shielding the site and, according to the doctors, drove a wedge of broken wood from the screen straight through Dr Elliott's heart.'

For a brief space Sir Stephen Rowandson remained silent.

'It comes to all of us, sooner or later,' he said at last. 'But I wish it could have come in a way different from this. A photograph? Yes, I think I can help. There was a photograph of Dr Elliott in our local paper, the *Standard*, only the other day. Come up to my house and I'll show it to you. Then, if you think it suitable, I'm sure the *Standard* people will be only too glad to lend you the block.'

Sir Stephen Rowandson led the newspaper-man into his study, where, almost at once, he apologised for the coldness of the room.

'I'm sorry to offer you such a chilly reception,' he said. 'But my housekeeper is away and I am looking after myself. However, we'll soon have a fire, and then I'll hunt for that photograph.'

Although the young man held out a restraining hand, Rowandson struck a match, and lit the fire. Then, crossing to a pile of newspapers on a small table by his desk, he began to turn over the papers one by one. But the *Standard* which he wanted was not there.

'Queer,' he said, 'I could have sworn it was in this pile. But warm yourself at what fire there is while I have a look in the dining-room. I sometimes leave the paper there.'

He went out of the room, and the young man looked ruefully at the fire. The edges of the paper had burned, but nothing more. As one last wisp of smoke curled up towards the chimney, the fire was out.

'I can't find it anywhere,' growled Rowandson, coming back into the room. Once more he went through the pile of papers on the table, and still without success. Then he saw the dead hearth.

'Oh, I am sorry,' he cried. 'The fire has gone out. I must have packed it too tightly. Stupid of me. But it's years since I laid a fire.'

Then a new thought came to him.

'And I'm willing to bet that the *Standard* I'm looking for is there, at the bottom of my wretched fire. I just took the first paper that came to hand. I really am sorry. But look! If you go to the offices of the *Standard*, in the High Street, they'll willingly show you the issue, and then you can ask about the block. Say I sent you. Really, I should have taken you there in the first place.'

With many apologies for troubling the Honorary Curator of the Museum, the young newspaper-man left. Sir Stephen Rowandson returned to his study and there looked balefully at the dead fire.

'I suppose I shall have to re-lay the damned thing,' he muttered to himself. 'I'd better do it now, and have done with it.'

Kneeling down in front of the hearth, he removed the coal, then the firewood, and finally the paper. Yes, he had packed it too tightly. But he had learned his lesson. Straightening out a piece of the crushed-up paper, he saw it was the *Standard* for which he had been looking. He might have guessed he would use the one newspaper that was wanted. Ah! here was the page that bore poor Elliott's photograph. He straightened the page. It was still a good likeness, even though the photograph was badly crushed, and a splinter from the rough firewood had pierced it in the very heart.

But all that held no significance for Sir Stephen Rowandson. He re-laid the fire, went to his bathroom, and there – washed his hands.

The Sweet Singers

The Sweet Singers

ALTHOUGH OUR SCOTTISH universities are strangely lacking in those facilities for social intercourse which form part and parcel of the life in an Oxford or Cambridge college, it may be questioned whether even those more ancient, and in some ways more fortunate, foundations have anything to equal our annual inter-university competition for the Professors' Challenge Cup at golf. Who first devised this golfing event is now unknown; and the 'Cup' itself exists only in the name. But of the popularity of the gathering there can be no doubt – save, perhaps, to the caddies of the chosen course who, though they may find our bags are light, are usually more concerned with finding our errant balls. For our enjoyment of the competition is not solely one of meeting old friends in pleasant places. There is also the game itself. And since the competition is played by handicap, with the handicaps assessed by old McIlwain of St Andrews, under some 'stone age' system of his own in which the average of previous scores is reconciled with age and weight and girth, even the very worst of us can still play his round in the hope that the final figures will show his own name at the head of all. Had it been otherwise, this tale would never have been told. Under McIlwain's assessment my handicap was 24.

Upon this particular occasion our meeting had been held at North Berwick; we had been favoured with a lovely day; and the luck of the draw had partnered me with my old friend Andrew Lomas, who then held the Chair of Natural Philosophy at Aberdeen. Not that the two of us said much during the round. Lomas played his golf with a precision and concentration equal to that with which he delivered a lecture or conducted an experiment; and I have a shrewd suspicion that in his secret heart he longed to reduce even golf to the neatness and efficiency of a mathematical equation. Over our eighteen holes practically his only comment was a dry remark about the importance of the 'approach' to any problem, and that came from him only when, after a masterly chip to the flag, he sank his putt on the last green to hand in a score of 73. But his handicap (McIlwain) was plus 10.

As it happened, however, both of us had decided to stay the night at North Berwick – I, in order to examine on the morrow a reputed short cist which had been discovered on a nearby farm; Lomas, because of the long journey to Aberdeen. And naturally both of us had booked at the old 'Royal', where we found that we had been given adjacent rooms, each facing the sea and each with a marvellous view of the massive Bass.

At first we had thought of an after-dinner walk to Tantallon and back again, but, with a cold east wind suddenly blowing in from the sea, we concluded that one round of golf was walking enough for one day. Instead we adjourned to the smoking-room, where the only other occupant was a somewhat stern-looking minister with a patriarchal beard and an undoubted gift of concentration – or, to put it another way, our ministerial fellow-guest gave no sign that our conversation in any way disturbed his engrossment in his book. What we talked about I cannot now remember, nor is it of consequence to my story; but about eleven o'clock we were both yawning and ready for our beds. And once abed I was soon fast asleep.

I had not been long asleep – or perhaps I should say that that was my impression, and it is a common impression and often a common fallacy in similar circumstances – when I was awakened by a gentle but persistent knocking on my bedroom door. Lighting the bedside lamp, I slipped out of bed and into my dressing-gown, and opened the door. To my surprise Lomas, also in pyjamas and dressing-gown, at once stepped into my room from the ill-lit corridor outside.

'I hope I haven't disturbed you,' he said, quietly closing the door. Then, without waiting for an answer, he walked over to my window, drew aside the curtains, and stood there, alert and assured, with his head turned slightly sideways, as though listening intently.

I moved over to join him.

'Strange,' he whispered, 'I can't hear it now.'

Not knowing what it was that was now inaudible, I strove to catch what sound I could. But all that I could hear was the light sough of the wind round the house and the steady beat of the waves on the sand.

'What was it?' I asked in a low voice.

But Lomas only motioned me to be silent; and so, side by side, we stood tense and expectant before an inn window overlooking the grey North Sea and the shadowy outline of the inhospitable Bass.

Suddenly I sensed that Lomas had stiffened; and at that same moment my ears caught the strange sound of a distant singing. The singing seemed to be that of many voices joined in harmony; but although there was this impression of many voices, the sound itself was little louder than the whisper of the wind and so faint that it came and went between the rhythmic crash of the breaking waves. Yet there was this also – with the singing I seemed to be no longer within the confines of the room but out in the open air and in the spaces of the night.

For some time we listened to the rise and fall of that strange singing. Then it ceased, and all was silence again.

'You heard it?' whispered Lomas.

I nodded.

'I knew it couldn't be my imagination,' he returned. 'And it doesn't synchronize with the wind, so it cannot be anything similar to the moaning of the statues in Butler's *Erewhon*. Shall we open the window? It is coming from somewhere outside and it may start again. But who are they, and why are they singing at this unearthly hour of night?'

I pushed up the window and we stood waiting, drawing our dressing-gowns closer as the chill night air came into the room. But we had not long to wait. Almost at once there again came the sound of singing, this time somewhat louder because of the open window, though also the crash of the breaking waves was likewise louder, so that again the sound came and went with the noise of the sea. But this time, with a start, I suddenly found that here and there I recognized a word, and with that I found that I was hearing (or mentally supplying) whole lines:

Yet, Lord, hear me crying,
To Thy mercy with Thee will I go.

But who could be singing that old metrical version of the 51st Psalm? Three more verses followed, and to the best of my recollection the arrangement was that given in the well-known collection by the brothers Wedderburn.

With the end of the sixth verse the singing ceased. Lomas looked at me with a query in his eyes as we still stood in silence, still listening and still waiting. But now only the sea disturbed the silence. The singing had come to an end.

Lomas pulled down the window and turned to sit on the edge of my bed.

'And what do you make of that?' he asked.

'Well,' I replied slowly, 'all I can tell you is that whoever they were they were singing the 51st Psalm and they were using the version in the *Gude and Godlie Ballatis*.'[7] And I gave Lomas a brief account of that interesting work.

'Humph,' was all his answer. 'We'll need to sleep on it. And that means we'd better get back to bed.'

He strode from the room. Slowly I slipped off my dressing-gown and settled back once more into my bed. For a time the singing echoed in my ears, and I still puzzled over the strangeness of it; but sleep soon intervened.

With the knocking of the chambermaid in the morning my mind at once flashed back to the singing in the night. Jumping out of bed, I hastened to the window and looked out. But the light of the morning offered no clue to the mystery of the night. And still wondering, I shaved and dressed.

There were only three of us at breakfast – the minister, Lomas, and myself – and at first neither Lomas nor I mentioned the strange singing. But when our landlord came in and asked, as a matter of routine or with a genuine regard for the welfare of his guests, whether we had slept comfortably and well, Lomas gave me a quick glance.

'You haven't a mission-hall near the hotel, have you?' he inquired casually.

'No, sir,' replied our host promptly, but with a sudden look of surprise.

'Well, it doesn't matter,' replied Lomas, reaching out for the marmalade. 'We heard some singing in the night, that's all.'

'Singing?'

'Yes. The 51st Psalm. Six verses of it, I believe.'

But our landlord only shook his head. 'Can't make anything of that, sir,' he answered slowly. 'And there's no guest ever spoken of the like before. It wouldn't be a ship, perhaps? Though a ship would be well out beyond the Bass and it would be nigh impossible to be hearing her crew. And why should a ship's crew be singing psalms in the middle of the night? No, sir. It sounds strange to me. But I'll make inquiries.' And nodding his head as if he doubted the result of his inquiries (or more likely doubted Lomas's questionings), the good fellow took his departure.

'Pardon me.'

It was the voice of our fellow guest, the minister, and we both turned.

'You have received a singular favour,' he continued, and his keen eyes, under bushy eyebrows, seemed to cover both of us. 'A singular favour. You have been privileged to hear "The Sweet Singers".'

'"The Sweet Singers?"' we asked in one voice.

'Yes,' replied the minister. 'And though I have long known the story of their singing, never have I had the assurance that their singing can still be heard.'

We waited in silence.

'Wodrow, I believe, has a brief note concerning it,' he continued, 'but there is a fuller and better account in the book *Jehovah Jireh*. One of you, I understand, comes from the University of Edinburgh. The book is in the University Library there. Perhaps it would be as well if you read for yourselves; for I could not hope to tell you the story in equal words. And yet I am deep in your debt; for now I have met two who have heard "The Sweet Singers", and I know that their singing will never cease.'

The minister had risen from the table; he walked towards the door and there turned. 'Remember. The book is *Jehovah Jireh* – "The Lord will Provide."' And with that he was gone.

Needless to say I abandoned my examination of the reputed short cist. Lomas and I returned with all speed to Edinburgh, where we at once made for the University Library. There the librarian soon put *Jehovah Jireh* into our hands.

It was a small book – a duodecimo is, I believe, the correct description – and it was clearly an account of the sufferings of the Covenanters in the time of Charles II. But it was not indexed. We sat down in the Professors' Room and turned over the pages, hastily reading the rubrics as we turned. And about the middle of the work we saw the heading for which we looked – *The Sweet Singers*.

'Here it is!' cried Lomas.

And there, with heads bent together, we read the following account:

Mr Robert Wilson being imprisoned in the Bass with many others did fall into a heavy sickness, and so did call for two others and did dictate out the rest of a paper which he had been before writing himself and did subscribe it before them as witnesses who also did subscribe, wherein he gave faithful and clear testimony to the work and cause of God and against the enemies of His Word.

Thereafter his discourse was ever that he longed for the time of relief because it was so near. His breath being very short, he said: 'Where the hallelujahs are sung there is no shortness of breath!'

That night he became weaker, but spake as sensibly as ever, and blessed those around him with heavenly expressions. And so began he to sing the 51st Psalm, but with great difficulty, and then stopped awondering and said: 'Will none of you join me in the singing? Even in the old version as it was sung by Master George Wishart[8] on the night that he was taken by his enemies.' Thereupon those around said: 'Sir, we will join with you.' And so did they sing again the first verse, even as those around Master George Wishart had sung with that blessed martyr.

The sound of their singing spread as with wings, and was heard by many more who in turn joined with their praise, so that as it were in the instant all those within the Bass had lifted up their voice in praise, and the sweetness of their singing reached out even to those upon the distant shore.

And in the end of the sixth verse he cried out with a loud voice: 'A singing of glory! A singing of the angels! Hosannah! Hosannah!' And so passed he from the singing of the faithful on earth to the singing round the Throne.

Nor shall that singing of the faithful in their affliction ever die. Two-score years have now passed, and in them have been counted five men in East Lothian who have heard that Psalm reaching out to them across the waters from the Bass. The 'Sweet Singers' shall yet be heard when the Singers themselves are no more. And the sweetness of their singing shall never cease but shall endure unto the very end of time. 'He that hath ears to hear, so shall he hear.'

We turned the page, but the story of 'The Sweet Singers' had been told, and the succeeding entry bore on a sermon preached in Maybole.

'Strange!' muttered Lomas. 'No one can persuade me that sound waves never die; or that if we could but "tune" ourselves "in" alright we should be able to hear the wisdom that was spoken by Solomon or a sermon that was preached by Knox. Science can find no place for fancies such as those. Yet we *did* hear that singing in the night. "He that hath ears to hear, so shall he hear." But how? That's what I want to know. How?'

I remained silent. And perhaps silence was the only answer.

The House of Balfother

The House of Balfother

'I SOMETIMES WONDER about those traditional immortals who live in secret chambers, like Earl Beardie[9] at Glamis. Do they grow older and older? Do the years weary them? Or do they live on and on at exactly the same age? That's the worst of legends,' continued Drummond, addressing the company at large, 'they leave too much to the imagination.'

'Well, if Earl Beardie is growing older and older, his beard must be mighty long by now, after some four hundred years,' put in Sharples, with mock gravity. 'Unless at some point in time, or at some given length, a man's beard ceases to grow.'

'I know nothing about legends. Scottish history is too full of them,' said Petrie, critical as always. 'But, if someone will give me a long drink, I will tell you of one "immortal" who was certainly burdened by the years – so much so that he had declined into something worse than a second childhood. Yet from what I saw and experienced, I shudder to think what "life" would have meant to him had he not suffered an unnatural and terrible end.'

Someone got up to provide the drink.

'It will have to be a long one,' Petrie added, quickly, 'for I shall have to tell you how I came to the House of Balfother, before I try to describe what happened there. And, after that, you will still have to hear the end of the tale.'

A very long drink was provided.

It all happened when I was a student at St Andrews – a 'magistrand', in my final year. And when I was also a great walker: which meant something more than the traditional ten-mile walk of St Andrews men, 'out by Cameron, and in by Grange'. To me, walking in those days meant striding across the hills by map and compass – the road to be taken only in times of sheer necessity – and never doing less than twenty miles a day. I can still do my twenty miles, but, in my student days, my long walks also meant trusting to hospitality, and hoping that the lonely farm or shepherd's cottage, marked with a small dot on the map, would somehow or other provide me with shelter for the night. Youth hostels were still unknown. Yet I was seldom turned away – even though, upon occasion, I must have been taken in at great inconvenience. And when I knew that that had been the case, I always strove to show my gratitude by giving any services I could on the following morning before setting out again – for I knew that any offer of payment would certainly be refused.

After the night of my strange experience, however, I left long before the day broke. And I was glad to be gone.

It was the Easter vacation of my final year and, faced with my examinations at the end of the coming summer term, I had decided upon a noble walk. I would take with me a copy of *Kidnapped*, and I would retrace David Balfour's route – partly that of 'the lad with the silver button', and partly that of David Balfour and Alan Breck when they 'took to the heather' after the murder of the 'Red Fox', Glenure. But I would do it in reverse, from North Queensferry to the Ross of Mull. Then back to Oban, and thence to St Andrews by train – to be at my books once more.

I had set out with high heart, and, blessed with fine clear days, I was well ahead of my schedule when I reached the few small houses of Kilchonan, on Loch Rannoch-side. From there I walked the mile or so to the Bridge of Ericht and then struck northwards towards Loch Ericht. It was hardly midday, so I planned to go up the valley of the stream, skirt the loch on its western side (for I would find no Cluny's 'gillie' to row me across), and, with luck, find shelter for the night at Ben Alder Cottage. I knew I was giving myself something of a task, for, according to the map, it was ten miles and a bit, with no habitation of any kind between Kilchonan and the Cottage. But I was in fine fettle, the day was glorious, and I had every confidence.

And then, for the first time, I found myself in difficulties. The way by the fast-running stream soon proved to be more troublesome than I had expected, so I struck up to the higher ground on the west. There I was beginning to make better progress, with a track to help me, when, gradually, the sun paled and the afternoon grew colder. I knew well enough what that meant. I knew that before long I should be running the dangers of a mountain mist.

Wisely, I decided to turn back to Kilchonan. And then came the mist: thin at first, but soon, all too soon, thick and enveloping. I knew that all I had to do was to keep on due south. If I did that, I was bound to strike Loch Rannoch – and Kilchonan – again; or, if I had strayed too far west, I would strike the road that ran from the western end of the loch to Rannoch Station. After all, I had my compass – a fine prismatic one, with a luminous dial, a legacy of my father's service in the First World War. More than once I had had to rely upon it amid the hills, and more than once it had served me well. But, although I could keep on walking in the right direction, I could not see where I was going; and, almost immediately, I was reminded of a new danger. Stumbling badly on some rough ground, I twisted my foot. Fortunately I was wearing heavy boots, but there and then I pictured myself, with a sprained ankle, trying painfully to make my way back and perhaps not succeeding, perhaps not being found. I took greater care, but, trying to pick my way slowly in thick white mist, over ground that I could barely see ahead of me, meant that before long I was chilled to the bone.

I cannot say that I was alarmed or dispirited. To the best of my recollection, my first feeling was simply one of frustration – partly that I had had to abandon my plan of reaching Ben Alder Cottage that night, and partly at the enforced slowness of my return to Kilchonan. But, as the afternoon wore on, and still I had reached neither Loch Rannoch, nor the road, I began to feel worried. Also, I was tired out. My slow groping through the mist would have tired anyone. But why had I made such poor progress? I had kept steadily south. Where was I? By now, too, although the mist was beginning to lift, darkness was taking its place.

And then, in the strange light that was half mist and half darkness, a tall square-standing tower suddenly loomed up a few yards ahead of me. Here was luck, indeed. Here I could find shelter for the night. Then came a strange sense of puzzlement, perhaps even of disquiet. What was this tower-house? It was certainly not marked on the map. There was no house of this kind anywhere between Kilchonan and Loch Ericht. But there it stood: a solid pile, much like a Border tower. It was no figment of my imagination.

There was no surrounding wall of any kind, and I walked straight up to the door. Again I was puzzled. The door was of solid oak, studded with iron nails. Surely no house still boasted such a mediæval defence? I knocked as loudly as I could, but my knuckles seemed to make no sound that would carry through the thick oak. Wondering what to do, I kicked the door with my heavy boots, and knew that the noise I made was bound to be heard. Standing there, cold and shivering, I kicked again and again. And at last my demand was answered. I heard the drawing of bars, the door opened slowly, and a man stood in the narrow opening as though to contest any entry.

'For why are ye makand sic dunts on the door?' he asked.

'Could I have shelter for the night?' I replied.

'Na stranger enters Balfother. It's weel kent. The king's writ aye has it so,' he answered, and would have closed the door.

But I was in no mood to be put off so easily, and, being young and impetuous, I thrust my foot into the gap.

'I'm sorry,' I said firmly, 'but you can't leave me out all night. I will be no trouble to you. I have food in my pack, and I can sleep on the kitchen floor, or in an outhouse if you have one. I want only that, and a fire to dry out my clothes.'

He seemed to hesitate, and then said again, almost as though it were a set phrase, 'Na stranger enters Balfother. The king's writ has it. It canna be.'

'But it must be,' I returned, and, pushing against the door, I edged myself in.

'Bide ye there, then,' said the man, seeing that I had indeed entered Balfother, and apparently not wishing to dispute my entry. He shuffled away in the darkness of what I assumed to be some kind of entrance-passage, and left me standing there. A minute or two later, however, he reappeared, carrying a lighted tallow candle on a dish. Beckoning me to follow him, he led the way up a winding stone stairway, opened a door, and ushered me into a small room. There he set the candle upon a rough table, and, without a word, left me again.

I looked at my quarters for the night, and again I felt that strange sense of disquiet. The room was perhaps twelve feet square and completely empty save for the rough table on which the man had set my candle, and a bed that was even more roughly made and was completely devoid of bed-clothes of any kind. The stone walls were cold and bare; as also was the stone floor. Only a small window, high up in one of the walls, and a crude fire-place in the wall opposite the bed, broke the forbidding monotony of stone. More than that, the whole room smelled dank and musty, as though the one window had never been opened, and the room had never been used, for countless years.

'A chilly reception, if ever there was one,' I muttered resentfully. 'Surely there's a fire in the house, somewhere.'

But I did my reluctant host an injustice. I had barely muttered my resentment than he came into the room, bearing an armful of logs. Again without speaking he laid them in a neat pile in the fire-place and went out, returning a second time with a log that was still glowing from a fire elsewhere. He placed the glowing log in the centre of the pile, lay full length upon the floor and blew until the log broke into flames and began to set the other logs alight.

At any rate I shall have a fire, I thought, thankfully, as I watched him at his task. And then once more I was puzzled. What was this house with an ancient look about everything? Who was this man? And why did his coarse clothes seem so odd? Had he inherited them from a grandfather, or a greatgrandfather?

As the man rose from his task, I thanked him sincerely for his attention to my wants. But he merely looked at me blankly and moved to the door. There, however, he turned before leaving.

'God keep ye through the night,' he said, and, with that, he was gone.

'And what might that mean?' I wondered. Was it just a benison, or was it a warning? I had virtually commanded shelter for the night, but what sort of shelter had I taken? What sort of a night was I to have?

Dismissing various vague apprehensions which flitted through my mind, I opened my pack and took out the spare socks, shirt and underclothing which I always carried on my long walks. These I laid, like a hearth-rug, on the stone floor in front of the fire, and then stripped to the skin. Standing on my hearth-rug, I rubbed myself hard and long with my towel. Then I began to dry out my soaking clothes, first arranging them in small pyramids before the fire and then holding them up, one at a time, close to the flames. I knew I ran the risk of singeing them, but dry clothes I had to have if I was to sleep without blankets.

For perhaps an hour I continued this task until all my clothes were dry. Then I dressed, ate some chocolate and plain biscuits, and felt completely refreshed.

I stress all this to show that I was fully alert and far from likely to 'imagine' things. Sitting on the edge of the bed I was ready to accept the shelter I had demanded and to face whatever the night might bring. Again taking out my map, I looked for a house somewhere in the hills to the south of Loch Ericht. No house was marked. But surely a tower-house like this was bound to be marked. What was this House of Balfother? And what had my queer host meant about 'na stranger', and 'the king's writ'? Well, I was ready for anything.

The fire was now burning low, but there was still life in the tallow candle. And then, just as I was debating whether or not to trust myself to the bed, and its possible vermin, I saw the door slowly opening. I flatter myself I was not in the least afraid. If robbery was intended, I felt in just the right mood to put up a good fight for my few pounds and pence. But it was not my host who entered. I was being visited by a large dog.

The animal, yellowish-white, and strangely devoid of fur, crawled slowly into the room and made straight for the fireplace and the warmth of the glowing embers there. But, instead of lying down, it *sat* down, much as a human would sit on the floor in front of a fire. Startled, I looked more closely at that strange posture. With a sudden feeling of revulsion, I realised that I was looking, not at a dog, but at a man.

He was completely naked. His skin was yellow, loose, and wrinkled – much like a piece of faded paper that had been crumpled up and then roughly smoothed out again. Soon, as he sat there, warming himself before the fire, he began to make little noises, similar to those made by a baby before it first begins to talk. After a while, he stopped and, teetering to and fro, began to croon to himself: 'Robbie Norrie, Robbie Norrie canna die. Robbie Norrie wilna die.'

It is impossible to describe my feelings as I witnessed this complete degradation of humanity. And, as I wondered what to do, the man turned, and saw me sitting on the bed. With a gurgle of delight, he got up and crawled towards me. Never had I seen, never shall I see again such an old, old face. It looked as though it had aged through centuries. Now too, as he came close to me, I could smell his body – a horrible, indefinable smell of rank flesh.

'Robbie Norrie,' he gibbered. 'Robbie Norrie.'

I strove to push him away, and his body yielded to my hands like a soft sponge.

'Robbie Norrie. Robbie Norrie,' I heard in a kind of childish sing-song as I feverishly struggled to avoid an approach that sent shivers of horror through every nerve in my frame.

I have no idea how long I struggled with that degenerate lump of human flesh. I was contending with a creature (for that is the only appropriate name) that seemed to have risen in bodily form from an age-old grave; a creature that sought to nestle close to me and that I pushed away again and again.

'Robbie Norrie, Robbie Norrie.' The childish repetition, as the foul creature constantly returned and strove to nestle against me, suddenly snapped my control. I seized him by the throat, and might well have strangled him, had not the door opened, just in time.

I let go my hold as I saw my host enter the room. The creature dropped on all fours at my feet; my host gave a sharp word of command; and the horrible thing, that once had been a man, sidled slowly out. My host, without a word, followed it.

I am not ashamed to say that I was in a state of complete collapse. I was a strong well-built youngster of twenty-two, and all I had had to do was to repulse a weak and decrepit creature, feeble alike in body and mind. Yet, somehow, I felt that I had been struggling with something so unwholesome that I myself had been in danger of corruption. Perhaps people in the middle ages felt like that about contact with a leper. I do not know.

As I gradually became myself again, I decided there was only one course to take. I had had enough of Balfother. I put my things into my pack and, creeping out of the room, felt my way about until I had discovered the stairway. I stole quietly down, found the door, drew back the wooden bars, and literally ran out into the night. It was still dark, but the mist had cleared. Again I struck south by compass, this time not caring whether I sprained an ankle or not. And, to my surprise, I had been walking for barely a quarter of an hour when I reached Loch Rannoch. There I stayed until dawn, resting my back against a tree, pondering over my strange adventure and regaining peace of mind.

My walk was over, save for the few miles to Rannoch Station. I caught a train there, changed at Crianlarich, and journeyed slowly, across country, back to St Andrews.

A week or so after my return, I received a note from John Barnet, my professor of Greek, inviting me to his house for tea. Term had not yet started, and the only other guest at tea was Duncan Mackinnon, the senior lecturer in History. I had told Barnet of my intention to walk from North Queensferry to the Ross of Mull, and naturally his first question was to ask me how I had fared. You can easily understand that my immediate response was to tell the whole story of my night at Balfother. But I was not prepared for what followed.

'Balfother?' interrupted Mackinnon, when I told of my arrival at the house.

'Robert Norrie?' he asked, excitedly, a little later.

But he let me finish.

'You know something about all this?' queried Barnet, turning to Mackinnon, when my tale had ended.

'Wait!' he answered. 'I'll slip over to my house and bring back a document which goes some way towards an explanation – though even then the whole thing is incredible.'

Mackinnon went out, leaving us to await his return impatiently – wondering what his document could be, and what explanation it could possibly give.

About ten minutes later he was back.

'As you know,' he began, taking a folded paper from his pocket, 'I have been working on the Fortingall Papers in the Scottish Record Office. And as soon as Petrie mentioned Balfother I remembered a queer letter under the Privy Seal which I found in the Fortingall Papers and which intrigued me so much that I transcribed it in full.'

He unfolded his sheet of paper, and although I cannot give you the exact words – though I still have a copy of the document at home – what he read out to us ran roughly like this:

A letter made to William Fowler of Balfother, his heirs and assigns, making mention that for the good, true and thankful service done and to be done by the said William, his heirs and assigns, in the keeping and maintaining of Robert Norrie, the man to whom the French leech Damian gave the quintessence in the time of our sovereign Lord's predecessor King James IV, whom God assoil, and the said Robert Norrie being still on life, therefore our sovereign Lord grants to the said William, his heirs and assigns, an annual rent of five hundred shillings to be uptaken yearly of the lands of Dall and Finnart. Providing always that the said William Fowler, his heirs and assigns, shall keep the said Robert Norrie close from all other persons whatsomever that he may be scatheless and harmless in his body, and that our sovereign Lord and, if God wills, our sovereign Lord's successors, may know to what age the said Robert shall live.

'Now you can understand my excitement,' continued Mackinnon. 'The date of that letter is 3rd April 1622. James IV died at Flodden in 1513. So already Robert Norrie had lived to at least the age of 109, and probably several years more – for the quintessence would hardly be given to him in his infancy. That had aroused my interest when I first read the extract; but, if

Petrie saw the same Robert Norrie at Balfother, as he seems to have done, the man must now be more than 400 years old.'

For a minute or so we digested this in silence.

'He *was* centuries old,' I said. 'I felt it at the time.'

'And what's all this about the French leech Damian, and the quintessence?' asked Barnet.

'Oh, that part is straightforward enough,' answered Mackinnon. 'We know that James IV encouraged the experiments of a certain Damian who believed he could distil the "quintessence" – not only to turn base metals into gold but also to yield an elixir that would prolong man's life indefinitely. James IV even made him abbot of Tongland; and, if you are interested, you can find the materials which he used in his experiments, and for which the King paid, in the *Accounts of the Lord High Treasurer* from about 1501 to 1513. My extract proves conclusively that Robert Norrie, who had been given the 'quintessence', lived to be at least 109. Is he still alive? At 400? What's more, when Petrie knocked at the door of Balfother he was told that no stranger could be admitted, and that the King's writ said so. Doesn't that mean that the same Robert Norrie is still being kept "close"?'

'We'll go to Balfother ourselves,' cried Barnet. 'And we'll ask James Waters to come with us. He takes so much interest in his anatomical reconstructions from the skulls and bones of men who have been dead for centuries that he's sure to be interested in the anatomy of a man who is still alive at the age of at least 400. All that puzzles me is how the affair has been kept secret for so long. Food – and even tallow candles – must be bought; and people are always curious about any queer goings-on in their neighbourhood. Surely the good folk of Kilchonan must know of the strange "creature" kept in Balfother. However, we'll see. I propose we ring up Waters and, if he's free, we'll drive to Kilchonan tomorrow.'

———·•✦•·———

Waters was free. And Barnet was a good driver. We arrived at Kilchonan about noon and, after a picnic lunch by the loch-side, the four of us retraced my steps up the high ground to the west of the stream that runs from Loch Ericht into Loch Rannoch. But we found no tower-house. Reaching the point where I thought I had turned back, we spread out, far wider than beaters on a grouse-moor, and walked southwards again. We met on the road by the Loch, and again we had failed to find Balfother.

'Are you sure you didn't fall asleep and dream it all?' asked Barnet, turning to me with a twinkle in his eye.

'I'm certain I didn't,' I replied, firmly.

'It can't have been a dream,' confirmed Mackinnon. 'Petrie had never heard of Balfother and Robert Norrie. He knew nothing of a letter under the Privy Seal – a "king's writ" – which banned the entry of strangers.'

'Well,' said the practical Waters, 'I suggest we inquire at Kilchonan. Perhaps we should have done so first of all.'

We inquired. But no one in Kilchonan had heard of a house called Balfother. One encouragement, however, did emerge from our inquiries. It was suggested that we should call on a Mr Alastair MacGregor, in Aberfeldy, who, we were told, was writing a local history, and who, of all people, was the most likely to be of help to us.

We drove to Aberfeldy, and we found Mr MacGregor.

'Balfother?' he repeated. 'Yes, there was certainly a tower-house of that name. It belonged to the Fowlers; but it was destroyed long ago. A grim and tragic affair. Come in, and I'll tell you about it.'

Alastair MacGregor did not live long enough to see his book in print. I can give you no reference to volume and page. But I am not likely to forget his account.

It appears that in 1649 there was a veritable epidemic of witch-huntings, witch-trials and witch-burnings throughout all Scotland from one end of the country to the other. And, in the August of that year, someone denounced William Fowler of Balfother, and Bessie Wilson, his wife, of keeping a 'familiar'. The 'familiar' had been seen. It was in the form of an old and naked man, who could not be clothed, and who ran about on all fours like a dog.

A body of men, headed by a minister, went out to Balfother. Apparently they had difficulty in gaining an entrance, but when, at last, they had broken down the door, had entered the house, and had secured Fowler and his wife, they began a search for the 'familiar'. And, according to the story, they found it – an old and decrepit man, stark naked, who babbled the words of some devilish incantation which put them all in terror until the minister cried out: 'Get thee behind me, Satan,' when they rushed at it and bound it with strong cords.

William Fowler and Bessie Wilson were burned as agents of the devil, and, with them, was burned their 'familiar'. It is said that William Fowler produced something which he called 'the king's writ', and which he offered in his defence. But the court refused to look at it, let alone accept it.

As for the house itself, after the burnings, the minister had preached a powerful sermon on the text, 'We will destroy this place . . . and the Lord hath sent us to destroy it.' Whereupon all the people had marched out to Balfother and, with crowbars and irons, had pulled down the house, stone by stone, scattering the stones over the land. And yet, apparently, the sight of good cut freestone was too much for the people of a later time. According to MacGregor, many of the stones of Balfother were still to be seen in some of the walls in Kilchonan.

We left the knowledgeable MacGregor and we drove from Aberfeldy in silence.

'What a horrible story,' said Barnet, at last.

'Yes,' agreed Mackinnon. 'One of far too many. Horrible. And yet,' he continued with his historian's eye for dates, 'Robert Norrie must have lived to at least the age of 136. Is that possible, Waters?'

'Certainly it's possible,' replied Waters, crisply. 'All the same, I'm glad that modern medicine has not yet discovered the prescription for Damian's quintessence. Old age is already a social problem, without further complications from an elixir of life.'

'But,' I cried, impatiently, 'can any of you explain how I came to the House of Balfother when the house was no longer there, and how Robert Norrie came to visit me when Robert Norrie had long been dead.'

No one answered me. And I know that no one ever will.

His Own Number

His Own Number

'WHAT DO YOU gain by putting a man into space?' asked Johnson, somewhat aggressively. 'Instruments are far more efficient.'

'But,' protested Hamilton, our Professor of Mathematical Physics, 'an astronaut can make use of instruments which don't respond to remote control. Also, he can bring the right instruments into work at exactly the right time in flight.'

'Maybe so,' returned Johnson. 'But what if he gets excited? The advantage of the instrument is that it never gets excited. It has no emotions. Its response is purely automatic.'

'Can you be sure of that?' asked Munro, from his chair by the fire. And, by the way he spoke, we could sense that there was something behind his question.

'If it is in perfect order, why not?' persisted Johnson.

'I don't know,' Munro replied, slowly. 'But I can tell you a tale of an electronic computer that was in perfect order and yet three times gave the same answer to an unfortunate technician.'

'Something like a wrist-watch which is affected by the pulse-beat of the wearer?' suggested Hayles.

'Something more than that,' said Munro. 'A great deal more. But what that "something" was, I simply don't know. Or can an instrument have "second sight", or respond to forces that are beyond our reckoning? I wish I knew the answer to that. However, I'll tell you my tale, and then each of you can try to explain it to his own satisfaction.'

———···———

As you probably know, when I first came here I came to a Research Fellowship in the Department of Mathematics. And, as it happened, one of the problems upon which I was engaged necessitated the use of an electronic computer. There were several in the Department, but the one which I normally used was quite a simple instrument: little more than an advanced calculator. I could 'programme' a number of calculations, feed them into it, and, in less than a minute, out would come the answer which it would have taken me perhaps a month to work out by myself. Just that, and no more. And I wish I could say it was always: 'Just that, and no more.' For here comes my tale.

One afternoon, being somewhat rushed – for I had been invited to a sherry party in the Senate Room – I asked one of the technicians if he'd feed my calculations into the computer, and leave the result on my desk. By pure chance the man I asked to do the job for me was called Murdoch Finlayson: a Highlander from somewhere up in Wester Ross. He was a good fellow in every way, and as honest and conscientious as they make them. I say 'by pure chance'; but perhaps it was all foreordained that I should pick on Finlayson. Certainly it seemed so, in the end. But, at the time, all I wanted to do was to get away to a sherry party; Finlayson happened to be near at hand; and I knew that I could trust him.

I thought, when I asked him to do the job, and when I indicated the computer I wanted him to use, that he looked strangely hesitant, and even backed away a bit. I remember wondering if he had been wanting to leave early, and here was I keeping him tied to his work. But, just when I was about to say that there was no real hurry, and that I'd attend to it myself in the morning, he seemed to pull himself together, reached out for my calculations, and, with an odd look in his eyes, murmured something that sounded like 'the third time'.

I was a little puzzled by his reaction to what I thought was a simple request, and even more puzzled by that murmured remark about 'the third time'; but, being in a hurry, gave the matter no second thought and dashed off.

My sherry party lasted somewhat longer than I had expected and, when I returned to the Department, I found it deserted. Everyone had gone home. I walked over to my desk, and then stood there, dumbfounded. Instead of the somewhat complex formula I had expected, I saw one of the computer's sheets bearing a simple number. A simple line of six digits. I won't give you the exact number on that sheet, but it was something like

$$585244$$

and underneath the number was a short note:

It's come for the third time.

I recognized Finlayson's handwriting. But what did he mean by that cryptic statement? First of all, he had murmured something about 'the third time'; and now he had left a message saying: 'It's come for the third time.' And what was that simple line of digits, anyway? If it was supposed to be the answer to my series of calculations, it was no answer at all.

At first I felt slightly angry. What was Finlayson playing at? Then a vague feeling of uneasiness supervened. Finlayson was too sound and solid to be playing tricks with me. I remembered his hesitancy, and a new thought struck me: had it perhaps been fear? What could that number mean? As a line of digits, a six-figure number, I could see nothing unusual about it. It was a simple number, and nothing more. Then, for a time, I played with it. I cubed it; but I was no wiser. I added up the digits and cubed the total; I multiplied by three and tried again; and so forth and so on till I admitted that I was simply wasting my time. I could make nothing of it.

Unfortunately I didn't know where Finlayson lived, so perforce I had to contain my curiosity until the next morning. Also I had to contain that vague feeling of uneasiness which still persisted. But the next morning, as soon as I had entered the Department, I sought him out.

'This is an extraordinary result, Finlayson,' I said, holding out the computer sheet which he had left on my desk.

'Aye, sir.'

'But surely the computer must have gone completely haywire.'

'The computer's all right, sir. But yon's the result it gave me, and I'm no liking it at all.'

'The computer can't be right,' I persisted. 'And your note seems to say that this is the third time you've received this result from it. Do you really mean that on three separate occasions, whatever the calculations you have put into this computer, it has each time returned this same number – 585244?'

'It has that, sir. And it's unchancy. I'm no liking a machine that gives me yon same number three times. I'm thinking that maybe it's my own number. And now I'm afeared o' it. I'm for handing in my papers and leaving, sir. I'll away to my brother's to help with the sheep. 'Tis safer feeding a flock of ewes than tending a machine that aye gives you a queer number.'

'Nonsense,' I retorted. 'There's something wrong with the computer, or with the way in which you set it and fed in the calculations.'

'Maybe aye and maybe no, sir. But maybe I've been given my own number, and I'm no liking it at all. I'm wanting to leave.'

I realized that I was up against some form of Highland superstition. Finlayson had been given a simple number three times, and that was enough for him. Maybe it was 'his own number' – whatever that might mean. I realized, too, that he had made up his mind to go, and that nothing I could say would dissuade him. Sheep were safer than electronic computers.

'All right,' I said to him, 'I'll speak to the Dean. And if it is any comfort to you, I won't ask you to operate that computer again.'

He thanked me for what he called my 'consideration', and went back to his work. I, in turn, went straight to the Dean.

'What an extraordinary business,' said the Dean, when I had recounted the circumstances to him. 'I wouldn't have believed it of Finlayson. I would have said he was far too intelligent to let anything like that upset him. There's surely something wrong with that computer. It's a very old instrument. Let's have a look at it.'

And, naturally, 'having a look at it' included feeding in the calculations which I had previously given to Finlayson. The computer quickly gave us the result. And it was a result far different from Finlayson's simple number, 585244. Although it would have taken me days to check it, the result was a complex formula like the one I had expected.

The Dean muttered something to himself and then turned to me. 'We'll try it again. I have some calculations of my own to which I know the answer.'

He went to his room, came back with his calculations and fed them into the machine. A few seconds later, out came the computer's sheet bearing the answer.

'Perfectly correct,' said the Dean, crisply. 'Finlayson must have been imagining things. Or else, for some unknown reason, he has three times fed a wrong programme into the computer. Even then, he couldn't get an answer like 585244.'

'I don't know,' I replied, slowly. 'He's too good a technician to make mistakes. And carelessness is no explanation. He's convinced he has received that six-figure number on the last three occasions on which he has used this machine. I'm beginning to think he did – though don't ask me why. But he's also convinced that there's some premonition in it. "His own number" has turned up three times. And "the third time" is a kind of final summons. Superstition if you like, but I'm beginning to feel for him. I think we should let him go.'

'Very well,' returned the Dean with a sigh of resignation. 'Have it your own way. I'll tell him he can leave at the end of the week. But you know as well as I do how difficult it is to get good technicians.'

We sought out Finlayson and the Dean told him that if he was determined to go he could be released at the end of the week. The man's eyes lit up at the news, and his relief was obvious.

'I'll away to my brother's,' he said, delightedly. 'He'll be glad of my help, and I'll be glad to be helping him. Not that I've been unhappy in my work here, sir. I would not be saying that. But I'm kind of feared to be staying. And if ye had not said I could go, I doubt I would have been going all the same. Though it would not be like me to be doing a thing like that.'

'Where does your brother live?' the Dean asked, quickly changing the conversation.

'In Glen Ogle, sir, on the road from Lochearnhead to Killin.'

'A beautiful stretch of country,' I put in. 'Do you know, I'll drive you there on Saturday morning if you like. It will be a lovely run. Where shall I pick you up?'

He accepted my offer with alacrity, and gave me the address of his lodgings.

I did not tell him of the two tests of the computer which the Dean and I had carried out.

⸺ ⦿ ⸺

The Saturday morning was fine and clear. I called for him at the address he had given me, and found him waiting, with his possessions packed into a large grip.

Once we had passed through Stirling and had reached the

foothills of the Highlands, the beauty of the country seized hold of me. Finlayson's desire to join his brother amid these browns and purples, golds, blues and greens, seemed the most sensible thing in all the world. The sun made the hills a glory; Ben Ledi and Ben Vorlich raised their heads in the distance; and, as we left Callander, the long-continuing Falls of Leny cascaded over their rocks by the side of the road. Finlayson's thrice-recurring number was surely a blessing and not a curse.

We had run through Lochearnhead and had entered Glen Ogle when, just as I was about to ask Finlayson for the whereabouts of his brother's farm, the car suddenly slowed down and stopped. I knew the tank was practically full, for I had just put in eight gallons at Callander. My first thought was carburettor-trouble, or possibly a blocked feed. I loosened the bonnet-catch, got out, raised the bonnet, and went through all the usual checks. But, to my annoyance, I could find nothing wrong. The tank was full; feed, pump and carburettor were all functioning properly. I gave myself a few minor shocks as I tested the electrical circuits. Nothing wrong there. Coil, battery, distributor, plugs, were all in order. I reached over to the fascia board and pressed the self-starter. The starter-motor whirred noisily in the stillness, but the engine did not respond. Once more I tested every connection and every part. Again I pressed the self-starter, and again with no effect. Thoroughly exasperated, I turned to Finlayson who had joined me in this exhaustive check and who was as puzzled as I was.

'Well, and what do we do now?' I asked.

'I'll walk the two-three miles to my brother's,' he said. 'He has the tractor, and can tow us to the farm. Then maybe we can find out what has gone wrong.'

'Excellent!' I agreed. 'Off you go.'

I sat down on the grass and I watched him striding away until he disappeared round a bend in the road. A little later I got up, closed the bonnet of the car, and took a road map from one of the door-pockets. Perhaps there was an alternative route for my way back.

I had barely opened the map and laid it out on top of the bonnet when a car came tearing round the bend ahead. As soon as the driver saw me, he pulled up with a screech of his brakes and jumped out.

'For God's sake come back with me,' he cried. 'I've killed a man, just up the road. He walked right into me.'

For a moment the shock of his words stunned me, and I stood irresolute.

'Quick!' he continued. 'We'll take your car. It will save the time of reversing mine.'

Without further ado, he jumped into the driver's seat of my car, pressed the self-starter and impatiently signalled to me to get in beside him.

So Finlayson was dead. Somehow I knew it was Finlayson. Dead in Glen Ogle where sheep were safer than machines. He had walked from my useless car to meet his death round the bend in the road.

My useless car! With a sudden tremor of every nerve I realized that the engine was turning over as smoothly as it had ever done.

Had the whole world turned upside down?

Mechanically I got in and sat down beside the man. He drove a short distance round the bend and then slowly came to a halt. I saw at once that my fears were only too true. Finlayson was dead. The man had lifted him on to the grass that verged the road. I got out and bent over him. There was nothing I could do.

'I saw him walking on his own side of the road,' I heard the man saying to me. 'And I was on my own side too. But he couldn't have seen me or heard me. Just when I should have passed him, he suddenly crossed over. My God! He crossed right in front of me! Do you think he was deaf? Or perhaps he was thinking of something. Absent-minded. How else could he walk right into me?'

The man was talking on and on. Later, I realized he had to talk.

It was the only relief for him. But I was not listening. Finlayson lay there, broken, still. Seeking life, he had found death. His 'number' had 'come up' three times. It was 'unchancy'. To hell with his number! What had that to do with this?

At the subsequent inquiry, the driver of the car was completely exonerated. In a moment of absent-mindedness Finlayson had stepped across the road right into the path of the oncoming car. The finding was clear and definite. Yet for me, I could not forget that the unhappy man had felt some premonition of mischance. He had decided to cheat mischance and seek safety amid the hills. And mischance and death had met him there. Yet what possible connection could there be between 'his number', 585244, and his death?

At first I thought that Finlayson had possibly seen 'his number' on a telegraph pole, or perhaps on a pylon, and, startled, had crossed the road to look at it more clearly. I made a special journey to Lochearnhead, parked my car there, and examined every bit of the road from the place where my car had 'broken down' to the place where Finlayson had been killed. But I could find nothing to substantiate my theory.

And why had my car so mysteriously broken down and then so mysteriously started again? Could it be that the fates had decreed the time and place of the death of Murdoch Finlayson and had used the puny machines of man's invention for their decree's fulfilment? An electronic computer that could be made to give the one number, and an internal combustion engine that could be brought to a halt. And why that number? Why that number?

That one question so dominated my mind that it ruined my work by day and my rest by night. And then, perhaps a fortnight after Finlayson's death, I was given an answer; yet it was an answer that still left everything unexplained.

I had gone over to the Staff House for lunch, and had joined a table where, too late, I found an animated discussion in progress to the effect that members of the Faculty of Arts were too ignorant of elementary science, and members of the Faculty of Science too ignorant of the arts. I was in no mood to join in the discussion, though politeness demanded that occasionally I should put in my word. The table gradually emptied until only Crossland, the Professor of Geography, and I were left.

'Neither Science nor Arts can answer some of our questions,' I said to him, bitterly.

'I know,' he replied. 'It must have been a terrible shock for you. I suppose we shall never know why that computer returned the one number to Finlayson three times. That is, if it did. And what was the number, by the way? I never heard.'

'A simple line of six digits – 585244.'

'Sounds just like a normal national grid reference,' Crossland commented.

'A normal national grid reference?' I queried.

'Yes. Surely you know our national grid system for map-references. Or,' he continued with a smile, 'is this a case of the scientist knowing too little of the work in the Faculty of Arts?'

'You've scored a point there,' I replied. 'I'm afraid I'm completely ignorant of this grid system of yours.'

'Probably you've been using motoring-maps too much,' he conceded. 'But the grid is quite simple. If you look at any sheet of the Ordnance Survey you will see that it is divided into kilometre squares by grid lines, numbered from 0 to 99, running west to east, and 0 to 99, running south to north. Then, within each kilometre square, a closer definition is obtained by measuring in tenths between the grid lines. Thus a particular spot, say a farm-steading or a spinney, can be pin-pointed on the map, within its numbered square, by a grid-reference which runs to six figures:

three, west to east; and three, south to north. A six-figure number, which is known as the "normal national grid reference".'

For a minute or so I digested this in silence.

'Can we go over to your map-room?' I asked.

'Surely,' he said, a little surprised. 'And see on a map how it works?'

'Yes.'

We went over to Crossland's department.

'Any particular map?' he asked.

'Yes. A map of Western Perthshire.'

Crossland produced the Ordnance Survey Sheet. I looked at it almost with reluctance.

Taking out a pencil, I pointed to the place on the map where, as near as I could judge, Finlayson had met his death. 'What would be the grid reference for that particular spot?' I asked, and wondered at the strangeness of my voice.

Crossland picked up a transparent slide and bent over the map. I heard him take in his breath. He straightened himself, and when he turned to look at me his eyes were troubled and questioning.

'Yes,' concluded Munro. 'I needn't tell you what the grid reference was. But can anyone tell me why Finlayson was given that number three times on an electronic computer? Or why my car "broke down", so that he could walk of his own accord to that very spot?'

The MacGregor Skull

The Narrative of the Reverend Finlay Robertson
by William Croft Dickinson
Published in the *Scotsman Weekend Magazine*,
Saturday 21st December 1963

Knowing himself to be a sick man, the late Professor W. Croft Dickinson, some months before his death, sent us this characteristic tale of the supernatural to maintain a long tradition of Christmas publication. It is sad to think that this tradition must henceforth be broken.

The MacGregor Skull

'IS IT TRUE,' asked Staunton, 'that the Campbells of Glenorchy granted lands to some of the tenants in return for a service of making war upon the Macgregors?'

'Well,' answered Henderson, 'I have certainly seen one or two charters demanding some such service, but I suspect they were exceptional.'

'And the Campbells had seized the Macgregors' lands, and were, in effect, fortifying themselves against those whom they had disinherited?''

'Roughly, yes,' agreed Henderson. 'It's a complicated story; and you should read "The Arrow of Glenlyon" as well as "The Black Book of Taymouth." The Macgregors, if you like, were unlucky. On the other hand, the Campbells undoubtedly had a knack of acquiring their neighbours' lands.'

'Aye, and there are parts where they still have an ill name,' put in Rennie. 'Yet they were not always the lucky ones. Let me go up to my room and I will collect a story of a Campbell who was worsted by a dead Macgregor, or so it would seem. As strange a story as you've ever heard,' he continued, making for the door. 'I'm not saying it is true. But it was written down by a parish minister.'

———·◦⟨⟩◦·———

A few minutes later, Rennie was back with a small packet of papers in his hand.

'They were in a copy of Rutherford's "Lex Rex"[10] which I bought many years ago at John Grant's bookshop,' he said. 'John Grant knew they were there, and had read them himself before selling me the book; and yet, good bookseller that he was, he insisted upon charging me no more for what he called the "Additional Manuscript".'

'We don't sell novels,' he said to me, with a smile. Maybe he was right; and yet maybe he was wrong.

'The manuscript has the heading, "The Macgregor Skull," and, underneath that, "Narrative of the Reverend Finlay Robertson," with, finally, "He being dead yet speaketh." Headings sufficient to arouse anyone's interest.'

'But any story about a skull should be interesting,' murmured Jamieson, one of our lecturers in anatomy.

'Yes. And I'm pretty sure you'll find this one interesting enough,' returned Rennie. 'Admittedly the Reverend Finlay Robertson's style is somewhat ponderous, and he uses few good Scots words – but then, as I discovered from the "Fasti," he was educated at Cambridge and stayed on in England for 20 years or so before returning north again.'

'However, I can whet your appetites still further by adding that underneath the text, "He being dead yet speaketh," another, and later hand has written in pencil, "A talking skull." And that may, or may not be true.'

'Go ahead,' said Staunton, looking round at us and giving, in effect, a general assent.

And here, from Rennie's manuscript, is an exact copy of the story which he read.

Narrative of the Reverend Finlay Robertson
He being dead yet speaketh

I HAD RECEIVED word from Sir Robert Campbell to wait on him at the big house. What business he could have with a minister of the Kirk I could hazard no guess: for Sir Robert was a hard man, reaping where he had not sown; a man of blood who walked not in the fear of God and who put his trust ever in his own sword and the swords of his followers.

But I knew that, once set upon a course, naught could make him change his way; and, with that, I knew his word was his command. Although I sore misliked the errand, I deemed I had little choice but to obey.

The darkness had already fallen as I made my way up the long road to the house. Nearing the house, I was surprised by an unwonted quiet. Here was no bustle of men and horse, no light or sound. At the door, itself, three times did I tirl at the pin ere I had answer; and while I thought that also to be strange, I thought it stranger still to hear the bars being drawn behind the closed door. Then the face of a servant lass peered out at me with startled eyes through an opening that was barely the width of a man's hand.

'Oh! it's the minister,' she cried; and I sensed the relief that came to her. She opened wide the door for me to enter, and scarcely was I across the threshold than she had shut and barred the door again. Then, coming close to me, she whispered, 'Did ye see the auld woman wi' the cairt?'

'I've seen no old woman, and no cart either,' I answered, with the wonder still growing within me. 'Who is she, anyway?'

'A witch, or a ghaist,' she replied, still in a whisper in which I could catch the fear that was in her. 'The laird couldna find her. And nane o' the men will be findin' her either, though they be out seekin' her through a' the glen and beyond. But the laird has the skull. And that's aye something.'

'Stop havering, woman,' I put in sternly, and myself exasperated by half-answers to my own wonder at the strange quiet of the house and my strange reception there. 'If you have a tale to tell, tell it plainly, that a man may understand it. What is all this you would be telling me about an old woman, a cart, and a skull; am I to see the laird, or must I first hear you out?'

And then, this way and that, and of a certainty to relieve her fear by the sharing of it, came the lass's tale. Piecing together what she told me – for her story was all disjointed and I had to bind it together as it went – I learned that shortly before my own coming to the house, and when the dark shadows of the hills were fast closing in, a woman's voice had been heard calling out from before the house, 'Are ye in, Sir Robert Campbell? Are ye in?'

Bidden to see who the woman was, and what she might be wanting, the lass had gone to the door and had there found an old woman and, standing behind the woman, a white horse harnessed to a cart.

'And deid men were on the cairt,' she said, fearfully, 'a' streekit doun, side for side.'

Frightened by what she saw, she would have closed the door, but, before she could do so, the old woman had handed to her something that was round and white, with the words, 'Tak ye this. 'Tis for Sir Robert Campbell hisself. It hasna' a tongue, but gin it talks it wilna lie.'

Hardly aware of what she was doing, she had taken what the old woman offered to her, and then, looking at it, had seen that she was holding a skull. At once she had dropped it with a shriek of terror; and her shriek had brought others, including the laird himself, out into the hall. To them she could say naught save broken words about a white horse, a cart that bore dead man, an old woman and a skull.

The skull was real enough, for all of them saw it plain, lying in a corner where it had rolled and stayed. And all, save the laird, had drawn back from it. But he, fearing naught, had boldly picked it up and, carrying it in his hand had rushed out into the gathering night to find the woman and to return her vile delivery – and, I shrewdly guessed, to seize her and bring her back for questioning.

But no woman could he find, and no cart drawn by a white horse. Yet there was but the one road and the one way for a horse and a cart to go.

Angry and perplexed, the laird had returned to the house, still carrying the skull. He had ordered the men to ride out and to scour the land until they found the woman and brought her back to him; he had stormed at the servant lass for taking such a gift from a stranger woman; and then he had marched off, carrying the skull to his chamber where he still was, awaiting the return of the men.

So much I pieced together from a lassie who, at the telling, trembled like a late leaf in the winter's wind.

'Aye, and no wonder you were sore afraid,' I said to her when her tale had ended, and she looking to me for what comfort I could give. 'But go you back to the women in the house, take up your Bible, and read there the 18th Psalm. Assuredly the Lord in His strength doth cast down and utterly destroy the powers of darkness and the works of evil. And that shall be a greater defence than the bars of a door. Show me the laird's chamber, and I will go in to him.'

———•◦·◦•———

I rapped with my knuckles on the door of the laird's chamber, and entered. The laird was sitting in his chair by the hearth and turning over a ruck of papers which he had taken from a chest that stood open nearby. Then I saw the skull. It was upright on a small table beside a case of books and, as I looked at it, there came to me an uneasy feeling that its eyeless sockets were surveying the whole room as though it were in command of all therein. Discomfited, I looked quickly away, and kept my eyes fixed on the laird and his papers as I stood there, awaiting his pleasure.

Sir Robert Campbell had undoubtedly heard me enter, but it was a two-three minutes ere he put aside his papers and deigned to turn to me.

'Come away, minister,' he said gruffly. 'Come away. I doubt ye will have heard of the auld besom that was here afore ye. Yon's the skull.'

I turned to look at the skull again, and this time I had the feeling that it was listening to every word. A sudden coldness ran through my veins, and for a second time I looked quickly away from it, yet telling myself I was no child to be imagining power in the bones of the dead.

'''Tis for Sir Robert Campbell hisself,' she says,' continued the laird, looking me hard in the eye, 'and gin it talks it wilna lie.' It talks right enough. I could take bodily oath afore all the Lords o' Session in Edinburgh that it said 'Ah!' contented-like when I brought it here and set it down. Mark ye, I ken fine where it comes from, but I'd lay out a purse o' silver to ken whose is the head.'

Without a doubt I must have shown my surprise.

'Aye,' he went on, 'it will be a Macgregor, one of those who were driven to the skirts o' Ben Buie and there put to the sword. I half-minded the tale when that crack-witted servant quean was deaving us all with her clatter about an auld woman, a white horse and a cart o' dead men. So I brought it here, and went to my papers where I found what I sought. It says here,' and he tapped on of the papers which he had taken from the chest, 'that, when the Campbells were for quitting the field, leaving the dead Macgregors where they lay neath Ben Buie – a curse on them all for a reiving, thieving clan – an auld woman came by with a cart and a white horse.

'Seeing the dead Macgregors, she stopped, and, auld as she was, set her to lifting them on to her cart, one here, one there. If she was looking for spoil, she'd win none, for the Macgregors were aye naked men. If she was for giving them Christian burial, bad cess to her – for there would not be one of them deserved it. Yet the paper says that the Campbells, daunted by the sight let the auld body be.'

'But,' I protested, and got no further.

'So 'tis a Macgregor,' he interrupted, grimly. 'A Macgregor's skull. And a skull that talks forbye. Faith, and I should be the proud man to be having a talking skull. Yet the skull of any Macgregor is welcome enough. 'Tis one Macgregor the less. More nor that, a skull carries no dirk. It cannot come at ye, silent-like, from the blackness of a gable-end. Yet I'm telling ye, had it no' said 'Ah!' when I set it down, I would have cast it out, or crushed it beneath my boot. But a talking skull! Man that's something by-ordinar.'

'But, Sir Robert,' I protested again; and this time he let me speak. 'The old woman who collected the dead beneath the slopes of Ben Buie must herself be dead these many years. That fight was in the past of long ago. How could the same old woman come to the house this very night? And if she did, then I tell you she's naught but the Devil's messenger, bringing the Devil's gift.

For a talking skull – if so it be – can talk only with the tongue of the Devil himself.'

⁕

And, even as I spoke, a fear plucked at my heart. The laird had received the old woman's message. He declared he had heard the skull talk. He knew whence it came. Then assuredly, if he was right, he must know, beyond all questioning, that this abomination and unclean thing had been brought to him from the realms of outer darkness by a woman who was long since dead.

And, if he was right, had Sir Robert Campbell, proud, godless and impenitent determined to pit his punt strength against that of the Devil himself? Nay more, had the Devil, in the shape of a Macgregor's skull, already entered the house to claim his own? Or was there some other, and less awful reading to it all?

I glanced again at the skull, and the fear that had touched me turned to terror at what I saw. The skull was grinning with a wide and evil grin; grinning as though it had read my every thought.

'O God, deliver me,' I cried and my voice seemed to die away on the words.

'Man, but you're a fine minister,' I heard the laird growling at me. 'Afeared o' a skull! And all the folk ye have buried in your ain kirk-yard! What becomes o' them? Skulls and bones. Skulls and bones. Aye, yon skull would make a grand sermon. What say ye to Ezekiel, 'Our bones are dried and our hope is lost'? Isna that a fine text for yon Macgregor?' And, so saying, he laughed brutally.

But to me there came a great shame, for I remembered how I had comforted the servant lass at the door. And now my own fear was like unto hers.

I hung my head, and the laird, seemingly weary of me, strode to the door and called loudly for a servant. 'It's ill work talking to a man in a dwalm,' he grumbled. 'I'll have word with ye anon, anent the new dominie to the school.'

So that was why I had been called to the big house! But I was too distraught to bring my mind to it.

The same servant lass who had opened the door to me now came in answer to the laird's call.

'Where are the men?' he demanded roughly. 'Send Duncan to me.'

Then he remembered. 'There's no a man to go with ye, minister,' he said. 'They're away up the glen. And though I sent them myself, I'm thinking they'll no be finding the auld body and the cart. Ye maun tak your ain gait home.'

He turned to face the skull. 'So it's the Devil's gift, is it. Ah well, it will pleasure me to hear what the Devil may have to say.'

Walking like a man in a dream, I made my way back to the manse. And all that night I lay restless, with the same questions for ever torturing my mind. Had the skull indeed spoken when the laird set it down? Had I indeed seen that evil grin? Might not both be fancy or self-deception, and nothing more? A skull was an ugsome thing. 'Twould be easy to think it grinned at me. Perhaps easy, too, to think it had said 'Ah!' Yet whence and how had the skull been brought to the house? There was the rub! And what had become of the old woman with her grisly cart?

My visit to the laird had been on a Tuesday – and the month, I should add, was late in March. On the Friday following I saw him come riding to the manse and, though courtesy demanded it not, I went out to meet him. He did not dismount as he saw me coming, but waited, seated on his mare, and let me walk to his very stirrup. Then, brash and bold as ever, he spoke to me. Yet even as he spoke, I could read in his eye that Sir Robert Campbell was fey.

'The new dominie will be Alastair Campbell, cousin to my sister's husband,' he said; and he spoke as though the office had been already filled. 'He has been at the College in Glasgow, and there, no doubt, has learned more than will be wanted.'

Yet despite that *ispe dixit*, I found myself giving instant answer. 'The kirk session and presbytery . . .' I began, but he cut me short.

'The new dominie will be Alastair Campbell, and, I'm telling ye, your kirk session, presbytery and all will find it so.'

'And since when has Sir Robert Campbell appointed the dominie to the school?' I queried sharply.

'Sir Robert Campbell has naught to do with it,' he returned, with a laugh, 'save only to ken afore ye who 'twill be. And how does he ken?'

Again he laughed, and I felt within me something that lay betwixt pity and fear.

'How does he ken? All he does is ask; and yon dried auld skull gives him the answer. "Gin it talks," she said, "it wilna lie." So I asks, "Shall I buy the lands o' Ballinferran?" And the skull says "Aye." Shall I raise the rents o' Auchterdennie?" "Aye." "Who shall I put into the mains o' Kettinch?" "Andro Sanford." "who shall be dominie to the school?" "Alastair Campbell." Man, but it's a fine thing to have a Macgregor's skull in the house, and to make it serve ye as a Macgregor should aye serve a Campbell.'

For a moment or two I stood speechless, prey to a wild torment of conflicting thoughts. How could an age-old skull give voice at all, far less give answers such as these? I had sense already that the laird was fey. Could it be that strange fancies were running through his mind? And yet there still arose that other thought, with which I had already wrestled. Who was the old woman? And whence had she come? Did some agent of the Devil already hold this man in thrall?

I found my voice, and cried out, 'Cast it away, Sir Robert. Cast it away, ere it leads you to destruction.'

'Cast it away?' he questioned. 'For why should I be casting it away? And your "destruction," minister, is no name for the raising o' worldly gear and heightening the fortunes o' my house.'

He turned his horse to ride away and, as he turned, I made one last appeal. 'The skull is the Devil himself,' I cried. 'What shall it profit you if you gain the whole world and lose your soul? Think how it came to you! Think what it is! Was ever a Macgregor like to bring profit to a Campbell? Oh man! Can ye not even think of that?'

But his only answer was to laugh at me and to taunt me with his parting words. 'The new dominie will be Alastair Campbell. Think o' that, minister, and think how I kent afore ye.'

Of the next few days I have nothing to record, save that the weather worsened and we had continual storms of wind and rain.

Then, on the Wednesday of the following week, I saw the servant lass who had opened the door to me at the big house. She came over to speak to me, and the word she had was that Sir Robert Campbell was like a man possessed – though that I knew for myself already. Never now, she said, did the laird ride out and about; never now did he storm and curse through the house. Instead, he stayed ever in his chamber, busy, it would seem with papers and accounts.

Yet, upon occasion, those who passed the chamber door would hear him talking aloud, though it was known to all that no one was with him. And already the woman folk were afeared of passing that way in the house. The men, on the other hand, were often out, riding to Perth and to Edinburgh – one had even been sent to Inveraray – and always they bore letters which were closely sealed. And the men opined that the letters which they carried were letters for the sale or the purchase of lands, for every letter was addressed to some man of law.

Questioning her somewhat, I learned that as to the laird himself, only the man Duncan had seen him these many days. For Duncan was ever the man of whom the laird called when he wanted aught – either food and drink, or someone to be ordered to be ready to ride out. Yet Duncan had himself confessed that the laird was a changed man. 'It's yon skull,' she had heard him say. 'It sits there like it rules the roost. And the laird aye looks at it like as it had a grup on him.'

Little more could I learn from her – save that all in the house were afeared for the laird and for the way that he was taking. More, and well nigh the end of this tale, I was to learn from the man Duncan himself.

<hr />

As I have said, the weather had worsened. We had had a week of wind and rain. The river was in spate and rising every hour; and old men were beginning to say that never had they known such evil weather to last so long. And, late in the night of the Friday, a week to the day that the laird, astride his horse, had spoken to me, and laughed at me, I heard above the wind and the rain a loud knocking and yammering at my door.

Opening it, I saw the man Duncan with the wet pouring down from him and a stark terror in his face that sent a chill through my every part.

I drew him in, set him down by the fire, and gave him a stiff dram. As he warmed with the fire and the whisky, he looked up to me and said, 'Minister, how can I find me the peace o' God?'

'It is waiting, freely, for all man,' I answered him. 'Put your trust in God, and He will give you peace.'

For a while thereafter he sat silent, and I wondered what was to be the tale he would tell. That it touched the laird and the skull I had no doubt. But what would its burden be?

Then slowly it came at last. And I learned why he longed for the peace of God.

That night, some hours past, he told me, the laird had suddenly stormed out from his chamber, had ordered his horse, and had declared his intent to ride to Balloch. All unavailingly, Duncan had striven to dissuade him, but the laird would have his will. And in one last and vain attempt Duncan had boldly declared that in such a spate the brig of Balloch must have been swept away, or would surely go ere the laird could reach it and cross.

At that, the laird had taken a hold of him and had pulled him into his chamber, steiking fast the door behind them. 'The skull kens a' things,' he had cried, and, facing the skull, he had called out to it in a loud voice, 'Will the brig o' Balloch stand?'

'And,' said Duncan, with the terror coming back into his eyes, 'deil a word cam out o' yon dreidsome mou, but the laird, wi' his een glintin' like ane dementit, cried out, "Ye heard it – aye, tae the verray keystane! And it doesna lie. I'm awa tae Balloch. I maun hae word wi' my kinsman ere the morn's morn."'

So the laird had ridden out. And Duncan, fearing for him, and unbeknown to him, had mounted and followed.

It was an ill ride, and only at whiles could he see the laird riding ahead. Yet, when at last the laird came to the brig, Duncan had a clear sight of him. And the brig still stood, though the waters were up to the very height of the arch. The laird galloped on and across; but, even as his horse passed the centre of the arch, there came a great roar and the northern half of the brig crashed down, throwing both horse and rider into the mad torrent beneath. 'And,' cried Duncan, looking up to me with a wildness in his voice, 'the ane half o' the brig wi' the keystane at its ither end, raxed out like to a gallows airm.'

As I said that is nigh the end of my tale.

Some days later, as the weather changed, I myself rode out to see half an arch with the keystone at its broke end jutting out from its southern pier. The brig of Balloch still stood 'to the very keystone.' If the skull had spoken it had not lied. But did Sir

Robert Campbell hear it speak those words? Then as I thought of the laird, I remembered his own words, spoken to me: 'It's a fine thing to have a Macgregor's skull in the house, and to make it serve ye as a Macgregor should aye serve a Campbell.' And I pondered over the way in which a dead Macgregor had seemingly served a Campbell; and the irony of it all.

Yet a minister must be allowed his 'Finally.' And, as so often in my sermons, it is drawn under three heads.

Imprimis: when it came to the appointment of a new dominie to the school Alastair Campbell was the only applicant and since he seemed to be well grounded and of good character he was appointed to the work. I myself was present and though I was much moved by the strangeness of it all I trust that my countenance did not betray me. And yet again was this but a coincidence and nothing more?

Secondly and stranger still: in the early morn following that fatal night when Sir Robert Campbell rode out to his death a shepherd tending a ewe and her lamb in the storm of wind and rain saw an old woman with a cart drawn by a white horse making her way across the moor where as he well knew there was neither road nor track for a cart to go.

Thirdly and lastly and most strange of all: when there were those bold enough to enter the laird's chamber no skull was to be seen there and no skull was ever found.

Notes

1. Page 16. 'Cairntoul' is apparently based on the real Craigievar Castle in Aberdeenshire. It is the scene of several ghost legends.

2. Page 61. Aeneas Sylvius Piccolomini, later Pope Pius II (1405–1464). A poet and scholar, he visited Scotland as a young man and met King James I.

3. Page 62. An incunabulum is an early printed book, typically one printed before 1501.

4. Page 89. Black Andie's *Tale of Tod Lapraik* is a tale of the uncanny by Robert Louis Stevenson set in the seventeenth-century Covenanting period. Dickinson had a strong interest in the Covenanters.

5. Page 89. 'Wolf's Crag' is a fictional name for the real Fast Castle in East Lothian. It is not to be confused with the real Wolf Craigs in the Pentland Hills near Edinburgh, where Covenanters field-preached and where the Sweet Singers were captured.

6. Page 92. 'Wodrow's *Analecta*' refers to *Analecta: or Materials for a History of Remarkable Providences, mostly*

> *relating to Scotch Ministers and Christians* by Robert
> Wodrow (1679–1734), a Presbyterian divine and historian.
> This book treats the period of the Covenanters.

7. Page 141. Gude and Godlie Ballatis: a very popular
    collection of religious lyrics from the early years of the
    Scottish Reformation.

8. Page 147. George Wishart (*c*. 1513–1546) was a Scottish
    religious reformer and Protestant martyr. On Cardinal
    Archbishop David Beaton's orders, he was hanged on a
    gibbet and his body burned at St Andrews on 1 March
    1546. The Cardinal was assassinated on 29 May, partly in
    revenge for Wishart's death.

9. Page 147. 'Earl Beardie' is one of the most notorious
    ghosts of Glamis Castle. He is said to haunt a walled-up
    chamber in the West Tower. The legend may refer either
    to Alexander Lyon, second Lord Glamis (died 1486) or to
    Alexander Lindsay, 4th Earl of Crawford (died 1453).

10. Page 178. *Lex, Rex, or The Law and the Prince*; *a Dispute for
    the Just Prerogative of King and People* by Samuel
    Rutherford, a seventeenth-century work which summarises
    the scriptural basis for Christian self-government. It had
    great influence on constitutional issues in Great Britain
    and on the Founding Fathers of the USA.

Among others, I am indebted to Peter Freshwater, whose article
on *The Christmas Ghost Stories of William Croft Dickinson* in
The University of Edinburgh Journal for December 2016
reminded me of Dickinson's excellence at a writer. In response
to Peter's encouragement, I undertook research on Scottish
newspapers and discovered that publishing a Christmas ghost
story had been a long-standing tradition for several of them;
in the *Scotsman*'s case since the early nineteenth century.

Another invaluable source was John Imrie's *William Croft Dickinson*: *A Memoir*, from *The Scottish Historical Review*, vol. 45, no. 139, part 1, published in 1966.

A.K.
2019

A Note on the Author of the Introduction

POSSIBLY AS A result of having lived in an old haunted house in his early youth, Alistair Kerr has always been interested in ghost stories and legends. Alistair studied Scottish History at the University of Edinburgh under William Croft Dickinson's successor, the late Professor Gordon Donaldson, who occasionally shared anecdotes about Dickinson. In the course of his historical studies Alistair became aware of Dickinson's importance as an historian and of his ghost stories.

One of Alistair's relations – a relation by marriage, he emphasises – was the notorious Dr Buck Ruxton, who was hanged for murder in 1936. During a Forensic Medicine lecture Alistair viewed some formalin-preserved parts of Mrs Isabella Ruxton (née Kerr), who was one of her husband's victims, although at that time he was unaware that they were related. A fellow student was Alexander McCall Smith, who became a lifelong friend and encouraged Alistair to start writing. This resulted in his first book, a military biography, *Betrayal: The Murder of Robert Nairac GC* (Cambridge Academic, 2015, republished 2017). Alistair has contributed articles to the Journal of the French Prefectoral Corps, the Royal United Services Institute's *RUSI Journal*, the annual journal of the Scottish

Heraldry Society, *The Double Tressure*, and *The University of Edinburgh Journal*.

Despite having taken a degree in History and Law, Alistair decided not to become either a lawyer or an historian. Instead, he served in HM Diplomatic Service from 1975 to 2009. He has travelled in Europe, Africa, Asia and Australia, has survived two coup attempts and a civil war, and has twice made the pilgrimage to Mount Athos. He is a Fellow of the Royal Geographical Society.